WHEN YOU LET GO

UNOMA NWANKWOR

KevStel Group LLC

Lawrenceville GA 30046

ISBN 978-0-9890738-4-4

ISBN 978-0-9890738-5-1(Ebook)

First printing May 2014

Printed in the United States of America

www.kevstelgroup.com

 Formatted with Vellum

PRAISE FOR UNOMA NWANKWOR

"Unoma sets up each scene in **When You Let Go** with an emotional punch that will keep your heart racing to the finish line. Warning: You will lose sleep trying to get there!" ~**Pat Simmons, award-winning author of The Guilty series.**

"I love how Unoma Nwankwor weaves the distinctive, spicy flavor of West Africa into her novels. I feel right at home with the food, pidgin English, quirky expressions, and cultural norms. I'm also enjoying watching her grow as an author. ~**Sherri L. Lewis, Bestselling Author and Missionary**

"In **An Unexpected Blessing**, Unoma Nwankwor has penned a sweet romance with an important message about love and acceptance. She's definitely a writer to watch." ~**Rhonda McKnight, Black Expressions Bestselling Author of What Kind of Fool and An Inconvenient Friend.**

"What woman hasn't felt the pangs of unfulfilled desire? In **An Unexpected Blessing**, Unoma Nwankwor weaves deception, cultures and the intrigue of love for a romantic journey that spans two continents and challenges the cornerstone of faith."~ **Valerie J. Lewis Coleman, best-selling author of The Forbidden Secrets of the Goody Box TheGoodyBoxBook.com**

"I read **An Unexpected Blessing** and I must admit I loved it very, very much. I look forward to reading your next novel." ~ **Diane Ndaba, reviewer Africa Book Club**

"**An Unexpected Blessing** is such a beautiful story had me over here in tears!"~ **Yvette Bentley of Words to Life LLC**

"Unoma's writing reads effortlessly. There is the perfect infusion of faith and international flavor. Readers are quickly swept up on a romantic literary adventure. **The Christmas Ultimatum** is a great read for anytime of the year"~ **Norma Jarrett Essence Best Selling author of Sunday Bruch**

"I loved it. **The Christmas Ultimatum** is my first read from Unoma and it won't be my last. I enjoyed the international favor she gave to the story. There is nothing sexier than a Christian man who goes after who and what he wants. Kudos!" ~ **Pat Simmons Award winning author of the Guilty Series**

To my husband Kevin, and my kids—Fumnanya & Ugo.
Because of them, I am.

Acknowledgments

To my Lord and Savior Jesus Christ. I thank you for paying the ultimate price that I may have life and for your grace which I do not deserve. Thank You for the gift of writing and I humbly pray I continue to be a vessel in this journey.

To my family, my husband Kevin who is my number one fan, cheering me along every step of the way. I love you and thank you. To my kids Fumnanya and Ugo, my gang, my pookies, my munchkins they keep me sane when insanity sometimes abound. I love you both more than words can express. I pray for God's continued protection over you.

To my parents and mother in-law, *Daalu*. Thank you for your constant prayers and speaking words of life, courage and hope upon me. Thank you to my siblings and siblings' in-law especially Emefie & Novelyn. You both rock!

To Mr. Emmanuel Ojeah. Words fail me in expressing my gratitude to you for all you have done for my family. Since I can't put everything into words, I'll continue to pray and think them in my heart...God does know the heart of man so I know He would get the message. May my good Lord bless you immensely for every thing. To my late father in-law, continue to rest in peace sir. We miss you dearly each day.

To my sistah friends from across the pond Lolia Oruamabo and Adamma Okonkwo, thank you for keeping me grounded and always being there.

To my new writing community, it's been almost a year since I entered into this arena with my debut novel, and it has just been a joy. The support I get from my readers is so overwhelming and I'm grateful to them. For those who took a chance and read my first publication...thank you. For those just joining the party...I appreciate you and welcome aboard.

To my author friends and sistah writers thank you, thank you. Sometimes support doesn't always come from the people or places you expect but trust in God and He will send the right people to you. A shout out to Michelle Stimpson and Norma Jarrett, these ladies have embraced me just because and I'm grateful.

Last but not least Pat Simmons, our late night conversations and emails feed my soul and make me want to be better at my craft. As you pour into me Pat, may God send people to pour into you.

Note from the Author/Content Warning

I am a romantic, a fact I'm sure you already know. I'm not just an ordinary romantic but a serious romantic. A good romance movie or book takes the cake for me any day. That's why my favorite channel is Hallmark. Thankfully my husband knows how to do the romance thing so...that's a conversation for another day.

This book however is everything but a boy meets girl story. It focuses on a married couple that is hopelessly in love so the romance is definitely there (one of my mentors told me it was so juicy) but it also deals with some very **deep issues of betrayal, illness, deceit, infertility and loss**.

I tried many times to put this book to the side while writing, but the Holy Spirit kept tugging me and little by little I got to the end.

I'm so glad I was obedient to the unction of the Spirit. A special thanks to my editor for pointing out things to make the story better.

There are some questions at the back of the book, so you could discuss them with your friends or just read through by yourself. If you have additional questions, you can reach me at www.unoman wankwor.com

Now kick back, relax, and mentally step into the world of
Amara and Ejike Dike.

Unoma

Prologue

It was 10:30 Friday morning. Chinelo Edozie wrapped her arms around her body as she paced the chilly hospital room. Her short, black hair was tied with a scarf that matched the flowing *boubou* that engulfed her petite frame. Instead of being in her office on Stadium road, she was here—Gwarinpa General Medical—for the forty-fifth straight hour. The hospital located in mainland Abuja was where she had delivered Obinna five years ago. That day, she marked her greatest achievement. When her bundle of joy was placed in her arms, she knew then that all was right in the world. Things might just turn out okay after all. And it was...for a little while.

Chinelo pulled the sheets over her sleeping son's body. With any luck, he would be discharged later today. She stroked his head. A tear rolled down her cheek. Obinna had been through too much in such a short time. He had been in the hospital almost every other month for most of his life. Her heart ached each time he was poked and prodded with the nurse's needles or had to shove down endless pills. Transfusion after transfusion – their lives revolved around his condition. Everything she held dear in life had been lost or stolen by this illness that just wouldn't let them be. Obinna was all she had left. She needed him to get better.

I'll do anything for my son to have a chance at a normal existence.

Something had to change. She had come to the end of her proverbial rope. There had to be other options out there.

She opened the door and peered outside. The hallways were deserted. The nurses that walked back and forth in feigned urgency—with shoes that alerted everyone they were approaching—were nowhere in sight. Finally peace and quiet, unlike the last two days. Chinelo closed the door and plunked down on the chair in the corner. She watched her son sleep peacefully as she bade her time until the doctor was able to see her.

An hour later, Chinelo was seated in the doctor's office located at the other end of the hospital. The beige color on the walls made the room feel cold while the harsh smell of disinfectant stung her nostrils. This was the last place she wanted to be, but it seemed fate had other ideas because she was a regular visitor here. Her shoulders slumped under the weight of her burdens. The man before her had been Obinna's hematologist for the past year. Obinna began seeing him when they moved to another part of Abuja after her divorce.

"Madam, we're looking good. His blood levels are back up," Dr. Ahmed glanced at the paper before him. He adjusted his glasses on his nose and looked up at her.

"You know that you have to make sure he eats the right foods and drink plenty of liquids. That will keep him hydrated and enable his blood to flow with ease, minimizing the chance of a crisis."

Chinelo looked at the doctor, her eyes saddened with disappointment. "Doctor, I can't do this anymore. I'm not trying to minimize anything. I need it to stop. Do you understand me? Stop."

There were several beats of silence between them. Dr. Ahmed leaned forward in his chair.

"Mrs. Oham—"

"That's Miss Edozie." Chinelo rolled her eyes. He knew she and Afam were now divorced. Why he insisted on calling her by her married name every time was beyond her. She had told him that she and Obinna don't share the same last name. She had bigger things to worry about, so she let the retort she had prepared slide.

"Ms. Edozie, my only other suggestion would be to get a bone marrow transplant."

Those words again. Bone marrow transplant.

"Is that the only way?" Chinelo's voice was laced with despair. "Is it a definite cure for Thalassemia?"

Dr. Ahmed hesitated. "A transplant from a matching donor is our very best option."

Chinelo placed her face in her hands and bent her head.

"We can test to see if you are a match. If not, I know you and his father are divorced, but surely he'd be willing to get tested to see if he's a match and possible donor for the sake of his son."

Chinelo started to sob softly. She had done this before. She was definitely *not* a match. And neither was her ex-husband. Her four-year marriage had ended after Obinna's last doctor suggested bone marrow testing. So Afam was a definite no-no. Their union had been a casualty of this illness that had put her life on hold.

"Madam, I know you're distraught, but it's a medium risk procedure." Dr. Ahmed paused. His phone rang.

Chinelo lifted her brow, daring him to answer it.

He heeded her nonverbal warning. He pushed up his glasses and faced her squarely. Over the next several minutes, Dr. Ahmed explained exactly what the procedure would entail. He did it in much more detail than the previous doctor. Chinelo listened attentively. She wiped her face. Why was God punishing her so?

Was this payment for living recklessly? Why was this happening to her?

"Mrs...Ms. Edozie, there is no need to cry. No need at all. God is in control," Doctor Ahmed said.

She shook her head and stood. *Funny how people keep mentioning a God that has shown me nothing but misery.*

Her deep brown eyes blurred and the room seemed to revolve as the reality of the situation hit. The vision of Obinna lying in that bed helpless flashed before her eyes. No more. She needed to make a trip to the United States of America. The cure for her son lay there. She continued listening to the doctor as he showed her brochures and recommended some centers that specialized in the procedure. She needed a matching donor and it was time she went in search of a cure for her son's illness. Why should she be the only one carrying this burden? No, not anymore.

Chinelo mentally began making preparations. Destination: Dallas. She chose Dallas for two reasons; one – her brother lived there and Gozie would not hear of her doing this on her own. The second was that she had loose ends to tie up and since she wasn't getting any help from the God everyone around her seemed to rave about, she'd have to help herself.

*A matching donor...*the doctor's words echoed in her ears again.

This time she was not going to be ignored. It was mid-April, almost the end of the school year, so the timing was perfect. All she had to do was get a couple of things tidied up. Like, take an extended leave from her Global Communications job and pay a couple of bills that would keep her utilities afloat until they got back.

Her son needed medical attention and she was going to fight to give it to him no matter the cost. Worry over other people's feelings or secrets being exposed were no longer a concern to her. All she cared about was Obinna. After all, everything would have worked out fine...if only.

She took a deep breath. The details were overwhelming, but she needed to get it together. First stop, the United States Embassy. She needed visas.

CHAPTER 1

T*wo Months Later*

Long before the sun made its appearance, Amara Dike woke up in a panic. Her heart was beating fast against her ribcage. Beads of sweat dripped from her face. It was only a dream. But it was the same dream she'd been having for days now. She turned and looked at the other occupant in the bed. Her husband, Ejike, was snoring softly. She rubbed her hands together quietly in supplication and thanked God for another day. She freed her legs from the covers. Moments later, she exited the bedroom and made her way downstairs.

Amara glanced at the clock on the wall. It was fifteen minutes before five am. She filled the kettle with water and sat on one of the bar stools near the island in the center of the kitchen. It served as more than a cooking space. She used the little nook in the corner for relaxation. She loved this area of the house the most. When the real estate agent showed them this house four years ago, this space was what cemented their decision to make an offer. She and Ejike saw the potential it had. With some work, they transformed it from a dark and dingy room to a bright and airy space. The tall, white cabinets with stainless steel fixtures matched perfectly with the modern appliances. The light brown and crème color on the walls complemented the granite covered backsplash and island. She loved the window that allowed her to look into the backyard. She had imagined watching her kids play while she did the dishes. But that wish hadn't come true.

A few minutes later, she was nursing a cup of chamomile tea as her mind wandered about the meaning of the dream she just had. Her mother-in-law had appeared at her doorstep with a young woman and a child.

I'm being silly. She can't just show up in Dallas without us knowing. It's just me. Ejike hasn't taken another wife.

She was his only wife. She had to keep reassuring herself that her husband loved her. Despite her childlessness, he loved her. No matter what her mother-in-law had to say about it, he wasn't taking another wife like most Nigerian men would after years of barrenness. He loved her.

Amara sipped on her now lukewarm tea. Her mind journeyed back to all the years of ridicule her mother-in-law had put her through. It started when they hadn't given her a grandchild after the second year of marriage. Six years in and it was still a constant battle, trying to convince the other Mrs. Dike that in God's time, they would have kids. Amara could understand her mother-in-law's anxiety—but not her cruelty—because some days she had a hard time convincing herself. If it weren't for Ejike who stood up to his mother, Amara knew she wouldn't be able to survive. That's why their appointment the next day was crucial. It had to work...it just had to.

"Father, please, you blessed Hannah and Sarah despite the odds. I'm expectant that you will do it for me," she prayed.

She emptied the remnants of the tea down the drain, washed the mug, and headed back to the bedroom. She didn't want Ejike to come down in search of her. He worried about her too much already.

Amara quietly slipped back into bed. Ejike shifted and pulled her close, but didn't wake up. She closed her eyes and snuggled close. She was determined not to let paranoia take over her life. But as much as she tried, Amara couldn't shake the feeling that even with the distance from Nigeria where her mother in-law lived, a storm was brewing.

THE NEXT DAY Amara sat in deafening silence. The atmosphere was taut like a new rubber band. The television hanging on the wall and the occasional swoosh of the door opening were the only sounds that could be heard in the lobby area of Another Chance Medical Center. The center was supposed to be a place where the hopeless were given hope of starting a family. But after two failed intrauterine insemination attempts, Amara struggled to hold on to her faith.

Amara squeezed her husband's hand. The smile Ejike gave her used to make all the difference. It always had a way of making everything okay. But it was no longer enough. She *needed* a child of her own. This was her last option—*in vitro* fertilization. Because her husband's smile also meant that he was serious about this being the last time they would go through this.

"Babe, we pray everything works out. But if it doesn't, we're done," he had said the previous night. "I've told you I should be enough for you. After six years, I've made peace with it and surrendered our situation to God. You should try to do the same. Besides, we could always adopt."

She had opened her mouth to protest to make him see it her way, but it wouldn't do any good. She had been trying for years to make him understand that adopting wasn't enough. She wanted a child of her *own* – one that would look like him or her. Their own child. She just shut her mouth and nodded.

"Amara Dike, Amara Dike," a nurse wearing light purple scrubs called for her.

Amara turned to her husband. "This is it, honey."

Ejike stood. "Yes, this is it. Let's go."

Amara and her husband walked hand in hand towards the nurse who was so engrossed in the file she was holding that she didn't see them coming.

"Good morning," the nurse said and looked up at them. "How are you all doing this morning? Follow me."

They strolled down a hall plastered with pictures of newborn babies and their mothers. Amara prayed that in a few months, their picture would be there as well.

The nurse ushered them into a room. "You can stay right here. The doctor will be with you shortly." Not waiting for a response, she shut the door.

Amara and her husband sat in silence. After a few moments, Ejike took her hand in his.

"Father in heaven, we give You praise for today. We thank You for this moment. We ask that You take control over the procedure. May Your will be done in our lives. In Jesus' name we pray. Amen"

"Amen," she whispered.

As though on cue, the door opened and Doctor Trickman entered the room. The fifty-five year-old man who had the build of a professional athlete had been her doctor since she started coming for these treatments. He came highly recommended by her regular gynecologist, Dr. Webber. She liked him. His sense of humor helped calm her fears.

"So how are we today?" Dr. Trickman flipped through her chart.

"Fine," they replied. Their tone was low.

"That's not the tone I expected. Cheer up. The hard stuff is over. Today we're at the final stage." He walked over to the sink and washed his hands. "Okay, let me explain to you what we'll be doing today."

For the next fifteen minutes, the doctor explained to Amara and Ejike the process by which the embryo gets planted into her uterus. Having gone through the stage of stimulation, egg retrieval and development, they were at the last step.

"You need to make sure you relax and let nature take its course," Dr. Trickman said. "I know you might be anxious, but it's important that you rest. I'm recommending a couple of days of bed rest." He looked at Ejike, as though waiting for a promise that Amara would rest.

"I'll make sure she takes it easy." Ejike looked at his wife and squeezed her hand.

"Okay, this is it. You ready?" the doctor asked.

Amara nodded.

He stood and walked to the door. "Let me get the nurse. Everything is going to be fine."

Amara nodded, her legs bouncing up and down unconsciously. She stared at the doctor as he left the room. She was thankful for his infectious optimism. It really would be fine. It had to be fine. Amara knew she had to have faith, but a part of her wished she could discern for sure that it would be.

CHAPTER 2

Ejike Dike smiled as memories of last night came flooding back. It had been a week since their visit to the clinic and Amara finally felt comfortable being intimate again. He grinned as he remembered how their bodies had swayed in a unique rhythm to a beat that could only be made from above. He was on top of the world and by the grace of God, he intended to stay there.

He tucked his burnt orange shirt into his brown pants and walked to the other end of his bedroom. He stood for a moment and contemplated wearing black or brown shoes. He opted for brown and sat on the edge of the bed to put them on.

Today was a big day for his career. His chance of becoming partner in Smitz & Dore Associates was dependent on closing this merger deal for a top name client—Neoh & Sons. The fact that he loved a good challenge was an added advantage to contract negotiations. The adrenaline rush he got when a deal closed in his client's favor was indescribable. Ejike considered corporate law his calling. He had worked at Smitz & Dore Associates for five years and had slowly climbed his way to the top. Life was good. He looked in the mirror and ran his thumb and index finger down his neatly trimmed moustache. After grabbing his jacket from the bed, he made his way downstairs.

The aroma of his favorite brand of coffee played with his nostrils. Amara's coffee always tasted so good. She was a lady of many talents. The kitchen wasn't the only room in the house where his wife displayed her talents. He snickered at the thought. The last eight years of his life had been pure bliss. When they got married six years ago, he was so unsure of what the future would hold for them. However, he was quite certain that whatever it had in store, together they'd conquer it. And that they did. A nice house in Dallas, Texas, two cars and very fulfilling careers. The icing on the cake was their relationship with Christ. They were blessed.

The beginning of their journey in Lagos, Nigeria was not as smooth as he would have liked it to be, but slowly and surely, Amara had introduced him to her love for Christ. He wasn't an atheist. He just didn't see a personal relationship with Jesus as the ultimate goal. But Amara changed all that. There was no other woman for him. Amara was his life—the bone of his bone. She was his African queen – independent, strong, demure and sexy all wrapped into one wonderful package.

Ejike walked into the kitchen. Amara was leaning against the island. She wore that smile that had powers of its own.

"Morning, honey." Amara sashayed towards him. She stood in front of him and cupped his face in her hands. She pressed her lips against his. Ejike wrapped his hands around her waist. She must have seen the look of desire in his eyes. She giggled and wiggled herself loose from his embrace. She stepped back and straightened his tie.

"Behave. We've got to go to work." She walked back to the island, picked up his coffee and handed it to him with a piece of toast.

"We got time..." Ejike's lips slanted up in a smile.

Amara was wearing the heck out of that power suit this morning. She had on a sleeveless, yellow blouse that showed her well-toned, butterscotch arms. The narrow, blue skirt fitted her curves perfectly, and stopped right at above her knee, showing off her shapely legs. Its matching jacket hung on the chair.

"I do, you don't. Remember, the people from Neoh & Sons are coming to go over the contract for the merger. Also, you have a meeting with Pastor Harris," she said.

"Hmm..." Ejike raised the mug to his lips and took a sip. The beverage was soothing. "Are you going into the office today?"

After working for a major public relations company for three years, Amara had established her own public relations outfit called Colab Relations. At the time, Ejike thought it was too huge a leap of faith. But once again, God showed up and showed out because most of the clients she handled followed her.

"Yes, but I have to go to the TV station first. One of my clients has an interview scheduled this morning. I'm trying to keep busy. The wait is making me antsy." Her tone was low, her eyes fixed on her shoes.

Ejike sighed and finished his coffee. He walked over to her and lifted her head with his finger.

"Look at me. It's just been a week since the procedure. Whatever the results are, it's going to be okay," he said. "Worrying will do no good when we've handed it over to God. He will do what He'll do, regardless." He kissed her forehead.

"I know, honey. I just want this for us."

"Have you heard me complain? God gave me you."

"I know that, but I feel incomplete not being able to give you what you want."

"What *we* want. And don't ever call yourself incomplete again. We're in this together. God's will be done." Ejike hated that she took their childlessness so personal. He only agreed to try artificial insemination and *in vitro* fertilization because she wanted it so bad. He preferred to leave everything in God's hands. After two failed attempts, he wasn't in favor of putting her through any procedure again. Soon they would get the results this latest try. Favorable or not, he wasn't doing it anymore. Ejike picked up his keys and started to walk toward the door. Amara followed him.

"I've got to go. Call me when you get to your office." He kissed her on her forehead and left the house.

~

GOD IS SO GOOD, it's ridiculous, Ejike mused later that Thursday afternoon. Things couldn't be any better if he had planned it himself. His meeting with Neoh & Sons went great. The final papers would be signed in some months in their Michigan office. They just had one more request, which he would work on before then. He turned his car onto Knott Avenue. He was on his way to see his pastor.

Ejike gazed out of the car window. It was a picture perfect, June day—sunny and bright. The streets were filled with people moving fast, preoccupied with themselves and their mission. These Dallas streets reminded him of his University days in Nigeria. That's were his love story with Amara began. It was love at first sight for him, although it took longer to convince her. Ejike smirked when he remembered the days of begging for a chance.

That first afternoon they met, he and his best friend Nnamdi Maduka had stopped by a local roadside eatery to cool off after a long day in the stuffy lecture halls. Ejike remembered being so thankful that it was his last year in school. He was eager to enter into the real world. He and Nnamdi placed their orders. While they waited for the food to arrive, their classmate Chinelo entered the eatery. Normally Ejike would have looked for the nearest exit to escape because at that point, he had run out of words in the English dictionary to make Chinelo understand that he wasn't interested in a romantic relationship with her. But that time, he couldn't let her be. She had just walked in with the most beautiful woman he had seen in all of his life.

Ejike invited the ladies to have lunch with them. Chinelo's eager smile reminded him of Nnamdi's words of caution when they had run into her earlier in the week. But when he looked at the other lady, he figured it would be worth it. She introduced the soft-spoken beauty as her cousin, Amara Dike. With her lithe frame and height, she could pass for a runway model any day. He loved the way her light brown hair shaped her angelic, oval face. She was his beauty to behold. Amara had transferred from another state university to get away from cult activity. The current between them was instant and electrifying. He knew then that she would be his wife.

With that thought, a piercing pain gnawed at him. It was always there any time he thought about what Amara would do if she found out about his one night of shame. God had forgiven him. He had even forgiven himself, but he couldn't risk Amara not doing the same. So he kept his secret to himself.

His phone rang, jolting him from memory lane. He shook his head and cleared his mind of the thought. That was all in the past. He hadn't heard from Chinelo again so there was no harm done. Besides she was all the way in Nigeria and he wasn't planning on going home any time soon. He looked at the caller ID and smiled. Just the person he wanted to hear from.

"Hi, honey," Amara's sweet, sexy voice came through the phone.

"Hey, yourself. Miss me?"

"Do you have to ask? Are you on your way to the pastor's office?"

"Yes, but I must have the worst luck. I'm in stand-still traffic."

"Oh, poor baby. Think about it this way, it's for a good cause," she said.

Amara was referring to the honor he had to lead the men's ministry in planning this year's couple's retreat. "Honey, I'm so proud of you. God has done so much with you – with us – in a very short time."

"It's all you baby. You introduced me to Him." The cars in front of him started to move.

"How did it go this morning?"

"It was okay. A bit shaky at first, but then my client caught up and nailed all the key points we went over," Amara said. "Oh, remember that lady I helped with her Easter campaign last year?"

"Mrs. Bryson? Yes, I remember."

"I got a call from her today. She said she referred another client to me."

Through the phone, Ejike could feel the pure joy seeping through her voice. His wife loved her job and it showed. "That's great. Greater is coming."

"Amen." A beat of silence passed between them. "Something weird happened today."

"What?"

"Someone kept calling me and hanging up the phone. It was as though they were trying to figure out if it was me."

"Why do you think that?" Ejike turned the steering wheel to avoid a pothole.

"Because the person waited for me to speak, then hung up." She paused. "Anyway, its stopped. I guess the person got tired."

"It's probably nothing."

"Yeah, maybe. You'd be proud of me. I didn't even think about the results once," Amara announced.

Ejike could feel her smile. "I'm always proud of you. Remember what I told you. God's got it, whatever the result."

He heard her sigh and mutter a faint, "You're right."

"Okay, I gotta go now. Then I'm coming straight home. Be sexy for daddy."

Amara laughed and Ejike snickered. She always found it funny when he referred to himself as her "daddy."

"Do I ever disappoint? Love you."

Two hours later, Ejike walked out of The Way Living Church. The final meeting with the pastor and the rest of the committee members had gone well. The retreat weekend was all set. They were going to a lodge in Treelands Resort located in Houston. Last year, the women's ministry had planned the occasion. This year, Ejike promised that they'd be outdone.

He glanced at his watch. Amara should be rounding up from work by now. Ejike decided to make a quick stop for some flowers before going home. He unlocked his car and was about to get in when his phone buzzed. He shoved his hand in his pocket, pulled it out, and looked at the caller ID. It was Nnamdi.

After the death of his sister's child, Nnamdi changed career paths and decided he wanted to become a pediatrician. And that he did. They had kept in contact with each other and by some stroke of luck, ended up in the same city years later. Their paths seemed to lead them in the same direction, except Nnamdi's path didn't lead to marriage. At least not yet. He preferred his life free from bondage—his allusion for marriage. Ejike got in the car and answered the phone.

"*O boy, how far now?*" Nnamdi asked.

There was something about the quietness in his voice that disturbed Ejike. He started the car and put the air conditioner on full blast. "*Nna, I dey oh...* What's going on? Why are you sounding that way?"

"We have a problem."

"What's wrong?"

"Hmmm...you won't believe who's in town."

"Who? And what did the person do to have you sounding this way?" Ejike laughed.

"It's not what they did to me, but what they are about to do to you."

"Who is it?" Ejike asked anxiously.

"Chinelo," Nnamdi said.

Ejike dropped the phone. A wide range of emotions swept

through him. His heart rate accelerated. Despite the coolness of the car, sweat began to fall from his forehead. His breath quickened. He wondered if Amara knew Chinelo was in town. Was she the person trying to call Amara all day? Ejike had a gut wrenching feeling that life as he knew it was over.

CHAPTER 3

By the next Wednesday, the client Mrs. Bryson had referred to her made his appearance. Amara was glad that she had taken extra effort in putting herself together that morning, even though all she wanted to do was sleep. Her polished look in her navy pantsuit and brown, leather pointed-toe shoes masked how tired her body really felt. She and Ejike had decided on a whim that they were in the mood for dancing and dinner, so they had stayed out late on a work night the previous evening. She loved that adventurous spirit about her husband. She was still reeling in the memory when the man seated across her spoke.

"Mrs. Dike, I was told you were the best and they were right," Devon Roberson said.

Amara smiled. She loved it when she had a satisfied client. The years she spent getting her journalism degree and building her media contacts here in the States was now working in her favor. Her firm's advantage over the big name firms in Dallas was her personal touch. She didn't use a cookie cutter approach for them all. She was proud of what she had accomplished. There was no way to explain her success except to acknowledge the favor of God.

After working from home for a year, she and Ejike decided that if she was going to be really serious about bringing in clients, she would have to rent office space. They had searched for weeks, but everything seemed to be out of their price range. Almost giving up hope, they decided to check on a last minute referral. And the rest was history. The developer of the office complex was eager to fill up the only empty space left. Amara jumped at the offer to acquire the two-room office.

She and her close friend Tonye had fun decorating. She had met Tonye Walker when she joined The Way Living Church five years ago. As the youngest members of the women's ministry, they'd bonded immediately.

For her workspace, Amara wanted a professional, but fun look. It was a public relations office after all. She wanted her clients to relax. The fuchsia walls were bordered with a black and white floral, vintage wallpaper. She managed to get a nice, solid cherry wood desk and chair set from a flea market. Her desk was decorated with fresh flowers and a black and white picture of her and Ejike on their wedding day.

"Please call me Amara, and it's my pleasure." She studied the man for a minute. When Mrs. Bryson called to let her know she was sending her another client, Amara didn't expect Devon Roberson.

Mr. Roberson was an ex basketballer. Everyone knew his story. He had a lucrative career in the NBA, but retired early after a trip to the ravaged country of Rwanda. When he got back to the United States, he formed a charity organization—Roberson Kids. Along with a couple of friends, they adopted two villages and one orphanage in Rwanda. The mission of the foundation was to provide the operational funds that fed, housed, clothed and educated the children that stayed in those places.

"Okay, Amara it is." His smile showcased his dimpled cheeks. He stood, shrinking the office with his height. He extended his hand and Amara placed hers in it. The handshake was brief.

"I'll write up the press releases and send them to you to look over." Amara walked to the door. He followed her. "Not only am I your publicist, but I'm also a fan. I want to commend you on the work you're doing in Rwanda. We need more people like you in the world."

"Thank you. I'm hoping the book sheds light on what's happening there and we can get some more funding," Devon said.

"I think it'll do fine. We'll get the right media contacts involved and things will move along nicely. I'll work on getting you speaking engagements as well."

"Wow! I did come to the right place." Devon placed his hand on the doorknob. "I hope to hear from you soon."

"You will in a couple of days. Have a nice day."

Devon Roberson opened the door to leave and bumped into Tonye. Tonye stopped dead in her tracks and devoured Devon with her eyes. Amara shook her head. She knew that they were about to spend the next ten minutes discussing how fine he was.

"Excuse me." Devon smiled as he left the room.

"Oh no. Excuse me." Tonye entered into the office and occupied one of the vacant chairs in front of Amara's desk.

"How did you get past my assistant?" Amara asked jokingly.

"Now, that is one fine brother." Tonye popped a piece of candy from the bowl of goodies on Amara's desk.

When Amara laughed, Tonye stared up at her. "Are you for real? So you mean I'm the only one that noticed that Shemar Moore look-alike?"

Amara shook her head and began gathering up the papers strewn across her desk. "T, if your right eye causes you to sin..."

"Look, I got a husband just like you, but that doesn't mean I can't admire God's creation. So whatever. You ready? I'm starving."

"Okay, that explains your attitude. You get extra evil when you're hungry," Amara chuckled and grabbed her purse.

"Hmmm. Are you all ready for our retreat? I heard the hotel is just divine." Tonye stood and adjusted the strap of her Michael Kors handbag.

"Yes, it is. I've seen the brochures and it's exquisite," Amara said.

"It better be, considering how much we had to shell out. Thanks to Ejike and his committee," Tonye put another piece of candy into her mouth.

"Leave my husband alone. You know if they had gotten something cheap you'd still have something to say." Amara placed her iPad in its case and put it in her bag. "Let's go eat."

AMARA CLOSED the door of her car and engaged the automatic locks. Lunch with Tonye was always fun. It wouldn't be complete however if they didn't stop and do some shopping. Tonye, who was a stylist, always guided them through the aisles to where the on sale, yet fabulous pieces were.

Amara looked at her watch. She had made it back to the office just in time for her telephone conference with another potential client – this time a child model, Samantha Richards. Amara was excited about this new venture. She was always up for new challenges and was pleased that the child's parents were taking a leading role in the ten year-old's career.

When she received the portfolio for the first time, she gasped. Samantha was such a beautiful, little girl. Amara wondered what it would be like to have a child. She rubbed her flat stomach with one hand and pressed the elevator's "up" button to get to her third floor office.

She thought about her husband and smiled. Ejike was her world. She wanted to be everything for him and make him happy. God had rewarded her for her faithfulness by giving her a husband like him. She was sure of it—those tithes, offerings, service in ministry, and fasting times weren't in vain. But the fact that she wasn't the mother of his children caused her constant pain.

Her mother and First Lady Harris always told her the story of Hannah and Sarah in the Bible. Amara knew those stories well, but it didn't do anything for the pain in her heart. All her friends that got married around the same time as she did had one or two kids. She knew the prognosis, but thought God would have turned her situation around by now. He did it for others, why was hers different? She had made every deal with God she could think of, but still nothing. Hopefully, He would change His mind in a couple of weeks when she got the results.

Several hours later, Amara washed her hands and opened the fridge to retrieve the lamb chops she had marinating. She used a prong to place them on a baking sheet. The evening news had just begun. Ejike should have been home by now. She tried calling him earlier, but her call went to voicemail.

She slipped her Wazobia Praise CD into the small player at the corner of the counter top.

Kai! This praise music reminds me so much of home. She bobbed her head to the sounds of the native drums emitting from the tiny speakers and worked quickly on the side dishes so dinner would be ready when Ejike did make it home.

Minutes later, she turned off the stove and headed upstairs when her phone rang. It was the same number that had played pranks on her some days earlier. She placed her blazer and purse on her bed and tossed her keys on the dresser. She decided to ignore the call. If the person was serious this time, they could leave a message. The ringing stopped, then started again soon after. Amara peeled off her skirt then sat on the bed. She sighed and answered the phone.

"Hello," Amara said forcefully.

"Hello, is this Amara?"

"Yes, it is. Who's speaking?" Amara asked with apprehension

in her voice. She didn't recognize the voice of the female caller on the other end of the line.

"Has it been that long?" the person asked.

"Tell me who this is…"

"Ah ah Amara. *E ma ro onye na kwu?*" the person said.

Ok, so the person knows me and is Igbo. Amara contemplated for a moment. "Chinelo?" She screamed. It couldn't be. She hadn't heard from her cousin in ages. "Chinelo? *O bu gi nwa?* Is that you?"

"*Ehen nu,*" Chinelo shouted through the phone.

The last time Amara saw Chinelo was during her traditional wedding in Enugu. Chinelo had been one of the hostesses that day. For some reason, after the wedding, Chinelo became distant until she and Amara finally lost contact.

"Where have you been? I tried your number many times, but never could get through," Amara said.

"You know Naija and their phone service." Chinelo said, using the familiar nickname for Nigeria.

"But then when it finally went through, the person that answered said I had the wrong number," Amara explained. "I even called my mom, but she said she hadn't heard from you."

Chinelo had been like the big sister Amara had always wanted. They were only two years apart and were very close. When Chinelo's parents had passed, Amara's parents had taken her and her brother Gozie in.

"*How far?* What's been happening? Last I knew of was your marriage to Afam right after I left for the States. So after all your *shakara,* you finally folded." Amara laughed softly.

Afam had always been what Chinelo referred to as her back-up man. He had pursued Chinelo relentlessly during their Youth Service days, but she never seemed interested. So it was surprising to Amara that right after she and Ejike got married, Chinelo married Afam. They couldn't attend the wedding, however, because they had relocated to the United States.

"Don't worry, my dear. *Gist plenty*. I'm in Dallas for a while. We'll definitely see," Chinelo said.

Amara sensed sadness in her voice. Then she heard the garage door open. Ejike was back.

"Okay, who are you staying with?"

"Gozie. You know he is here," Chinelo said.

"Really? I thought he lived in Canada?"

"Yes, but he relocated some months ago."

Amara was never close to Gozie. He was a lot older than her and Chinelo, so was always distant.

"We have to see each other soon. Ejike will be so shocked to know you just surfaced," Amara said. She made her way to the landing just in time to see Ejike coming up the stairs.

His eyebrows were scrunched together. He looked tired and weary. He had been this way for the last week. Something was bothering him, but he told her it was just work stress. He walked towards her and wrapped his arms around her. His hug was tighter than usual. She almost felt her air being cut off. When he let go, Amara caressed his cheek with her free hand.

"Chi, text me your address. My baby is back and he needs attention," Amara giggled, referring to Chinelo by her nickname. She felt Ejike tense.

"Lucky you. Okay, I'll let you go. Say hi to Ejike for me."

Amara hung up the phone. Stepping out of Ejike's embrace, she looked up at him.

"What's wrong, honey?"

"Who was that on the phone?" Ejike asked.

Amara noticed he ignored her question. He seemed to shut down a lot lately, but she wasn't having it today. "I asked you a question. What's wrong? Come here." Amara took her husband's hand and led him to the bedroom.

He sat on the bed and she stood in front of him. Ejike wrapped his arms around her waist and placed his head against her stomach.

Amara tossed her phone on the bed and rubbed his head. After a brief silence, she asked again. "So, what's wrong?"

"Nothing, my love. I'm just tired. It's been a hard day. A good day, but a hard one still," Ejike said. "Who was that on the phone?"

"You wouldn't believe it if I told you." She paused. "It was Chinelo. She's in Dallas."

She saw his jaw tighten, and then he smiled a phony smile that didn't reach his eyes. Amara didn't know what happened between Ejike and Chinelo. It was Chinelo that introduced her to him in the first place. One minute they were buddies and the next, he just stopped liking her. He didn't say it in so many words, but Amara knew him. His attitude changed towards Chinelo. Amara never pushed it since both of them always seemed to say, "nothing's wrong" whenever she asked.

"That's nice. How long is she here for?" Ejike asked.

"I don't know yet. Hopefully, I'll be meeting with her soon." Amara pulled off her earrings and placed them on the dresser.

"Oh, okay, cool." Ejike took his shirt out of his pants and unbuttoned it. "What has she been up to?"

"I have no idea, but I'll find out once we *gist*." Amara said, referring to their upcoming gossip session. She studied her husband for a few seconds. "Dinner is ready. Let's go eat and then I'll run a relaxing bath for us." She kissed his head and walked to the chair to get her robe.

An hour later, Amara and Ejike were done with dinner. The kitchen had been restored to its normal state and Ejike was taking out the trash.

"Are you still up for that bath?" Amara shouted from the bathroom. She turned on the faucet and began to run the water. She turned around and bumped into her husband. He steadied her.

"A soak in the tub with you? You know you don't have to ask me twice." He kissed her hard on the lips at first. Then he deepened the kiss with urgency.

Amara became weak in the knees—his kiss always did that to her. She wrapped her arms around his neck. "You better stop or we'll never take that bath." She broke away and turned to light some candles.

Ejike dimmed the lights. "Okay, I'll stop...but only for now. I need you tonight, baby." His baritone voice lowered an octave. His eyes narrowed.

Amara felt like he was devouring her already. She smiled and let her robe fall to the floor. "Then me you shall have." She winked and stepped into the bathtub. Ejike followed into her open arms.

CHAPTER 4

The sunlight peered through the curtains of their massive master bedroom. Ejike stirred between the sheets, careful not to wake Amara. He relished in the peaceful look on her face as she slept. He lived for that smile. He had promised to make her happy all the days of her life. Child or no child, he was content that she was his.

Nine days had passed since he heard Chinelo was in town. His instincts told him there was trouble looming. He looked to the ceiling and whispered softly, "Lord, please I need help in the coming days to keep my promise to make her happy."

Amara must have heard him because she moved. The silk scarf wrapped around her head shifted. She smiled at him. "Good morning, honey," she said.

"Good morning, babe. Did you sleep well?"

"For the little time you let me, I did." She snuggled close to him.

Ejike raised his brow. "I didn't hear you complaining last night."

"Complain *ke*? Never."

"So, what do you have planned for today?" Ejike kissed her on her forehead and sat up.

"Uh, nothing really. Need to go to the store, run a few errands, and then come back home to cook," Amara said.

"I coach the boys this morning, and then I plan on coming home and keeping my baby company." Ejike smiled sheepishly as he began to caress his wife's body.

"Don't start because you'll be late," Amara laughed as she slid underneath the covers.

"Where are you running to?" Ejike grinned and followed her.

A couple of hours later, Ejike stepped out of the shower with a towel wrapped around his waist.

"You are fine *sha...kai*!" Amara swatted her husband on his buttocks on her way to the bathroom.

Ejike laughed and began to get ready. If he didn't hurry, he'd be late. Nnamdi had already sent him a text reminding him of the time. He did that every coaching session because of what he called Ejike's loyalty to African time.

About two years ago, they had signed up to coach soccer at the local community center. It was fulfilling for them to mentor as well during these sessions. Some of these boys didn't have father figures in their lives and being able to provide the little emotional support they could was worthwhile. Although Amara was supportive and loved to hear stories about the boys, Ejike tried not to talk much about them. He was careful not to do anything that would remind her of their childlessness.

By the time Amara re-entered the room, Ejike was sitting on the bed lacing up his sneakers.

"I thought you were going to sleep in there." He got up from the bed and walked to the dresser. One his way, he swatted her on her buttocks, returning the favor.

"Ouch." Amara took off her shower cap, secured her towel around her breasts, and squeezed some lotion into her hands.

Ejike looked around to make sure he wasn't forgetting

anything. He walked to Amara and kissed her on the cheek. "All right, babe. I'm leaving. I might stop at Nnamdi's for a bit on my way back." He picked up his keys from the dresser.

"Ok, I'll soon leave the house myself. Won't you eat anything? Just give me a minute." She rubbed lotion on her legs.

"You forgot we always have breakfast with the boys after practice."

"Oh yeah, okay. See you later."

Ejike thought he was home free until Amara called him back. If his hunch was correct, she wanted to talk about Chinelo. He had successfully avoided the topic the last couple of days.

"Yeah, what's up?"

"Be nice to Chinelo when she comes here."

"I'm always nice."

"No, you aren't. Remember, she was instrumental in bringing us together. If this is about Udo—God rest his soul—they both weren't ready for a commitment."

Ejike had no idea how Amara drew that conclusion. His cousin, Udo, had nothing to do with his issues with Chinelo. But if that's what she thought, he would let her. At least 'til he understood the nature of Chinelo's visit. Her cousin wasn't all Amara thought she was.

"Babe, I gotta go. I'll be good." He kissed her lips and left.

"MR. D, I don't wanna be getting in trouble. That's why I tell my mama a lie," Cole said. He was a nine year-old boy whom Ejike had a special spot in his heart for. At the beginning of the year when Ejike started coaching a new set of boys, he was drawn to Cole immediately. He was the middle child of three boys. His father disappeared with another woman when the last child was just three months old.

Ejike cleared his throat and picked up his glass of orange juice.

After practicing for two hours, he, Nnamdi and two other coaches brought the boys to IHOP. Before any boy was allowed to go on these breakfast trips they had to get parental or a guardian's consent.

"Err... I think you should still tell her, little man. She loves you, so even if she does discipline you, it'll be in love," Ejike took a sip from his glass.

"If you say so, but I don't want no whipping." Cole took a bite of his sausage.

Ejike stretched his hands and rubbed Cole's head. "But I don't want *a* whipping." Ejike corrected the boy. "And trust me. I say so, because when you keep a lie, it keeps getting bigger."

Nnamdi smirked "You don't say?" He raised his glass and took a long drink of his juice.

Ejike recognized Nnamdi's sarcasm. Over the years, Nnamdi had gotten on him about coming clean with Amara.

Cole looked at Ejike, then at Nnamdi. He had a confused look on his face. "So I shouldn't tell her?"

"Don't listen to him." Ejike ignored Nnamdi's inference to the lie that Ejike had been living.

Cole nodded and joined the other boys in discussing the latest Disney movie. Ejike slipped into a comfortable silence as he anticipated Chinelo's next move.

A LITTLE WHILE LATER, after all the boys had been picked up from the center, Ejike stretched his legs on the ottoman in the center of his friend's living room.

"I have no idea why she's in the U.S, but I know it can't be good," Ejike said.

He and Nnamdi hadn't had a chance to *really* talk since Chinelo's appearance in Dallas.

"Man, get your feet off my furniture. I know Amara don't play like that." Nnamdi used his arm to move his friend's legs. Then he handed Ejike a cold bottle of water and sat on the adjacent chair.

"My bad."

"Don't get so worked up. For all you know, Chinelo might just be here on vacation and isn't even concerned about you."

"Yeah, you might be right." Ejike took a sip of his water and placed the bottle on the coaster nearby. "Besides, what's it been? Six years?"

"She's married, you're married. Since you didn't tell Amara all those years ago when I told you to, she doesn't have to know anything now. It's all good. Stop worrying," Nnamdi said.

"How could I be so stupid, man? I let my guard down. In school, when Amara began to suspect as well that her cousin liked me, I thought I handled it by introducing Chinelo to Udo."

"Man, please. A desperate woman will find a way by any means necessary."

"If Amara ever finds out about Chinelo and I, all hell will break loose. I love her man. That can't happen."

"Then you should have kept your pants zipped." Nnamdi laughed, but his friend didn't join in. "My bad. Just relax."

After a brief pause, Nnamdi asked, "Has she contacted Amara?"

"Yes, I came back home one day and they were on the phone. I was so glad when Amara lost her contact information all these years ago."

"Just play it cool. Don't say anything. When and if she does start trouble, then you'll know your next move." Nnamdi stood and made his way to the mantle to get the remote control. He tossed it to Ejike. "Here, watch some TV while I go shower. I've got some errands to run." Nnamdi headed towards the staircase.

Ejike idly turned on the television while his mind went back to the year that was supposed to be the happiest of his life. The year that everything changed. He remembered that cool, November night. The grey skies and threat of rain should have been a sign that what Amara was about to tell him wouldn't be good. He hadn't seen her for weeks. She'd been having severe abdominal pain, so the doctor had recommended a hysteroscopy. She was diagnosed with severe endometriosis, which caused blockage of one of her fallopian tubes. The prognosis was that it would be difficult for her to bear children. He had tried to help her see that everything would be all right, but Amara became depressed and he felt like she was slipping away from him. She changed from the person he knew, shutting him out completely. His aim of going to her house that day was to put a stop to the madness. They were supposed to be married in eight weeks.

"Ejike, I don't want to be married to you and not be able to give you a child. I won't be able to stand the pressure from your people." Amara said.

"It takes two to make children—"

"You know that, I know that, but don't even kid yourself into thinking that your mom will see it the same way." Amara put her hands on her hips. "You see, I like this my small life, free of wahala."

"So what I want doesn't matter?" Ejike paced back and forth.

"Ejike, my love, it does. But I don't want to subject you to a lifetime of having to settle misunderstandings between your mom and I."

"Amara, you're not making sense. Do you love me?"

"How can you even ask such? Of course I do—"

"You're not acting like it...I've told you, I love you and I don't care. Besides, at the risk of sounding like a broken record, the doctors don't have the final say. God does."

Amara remained silent.

Ejike was angered. "I'm done chasing after you. You have to trust and believe in my love for you. If not, then there is nothing for us to build on." He walked to the door. "When you make up your mind, let me know." He opened the door and walked out.

. . .

"You ready to head out?" Nnamdi's voice jolted Ejike back to the present.

Ejike stood and patted his pocket for his keys. "Yeah, I'm ready."

"Man, go home to your wife. You're most likely stressing for nothing."

Ejike sighed. He hoped Nnamdi was right.

His thoughts went back to that night that Amara had broken off their engagement. Against his better judgment, he had headed straight for a bar. Amara moved to Enugu shortly after to be with her parents. And so began his frequent trips to bars and night-clubs. Anything to escape the pain of his shattered heart. Chinelo became his confidant as he tried to figure his life out. When he was with her, he felt close to Amara. All they did was talk and hang out. Until one night he had a lapse in judgment. That decision had held him captive for six years.

CHAPTER 5

Amara smiled, satisfied with the spread in front of her. She had spent the better part of the morning at the farmer's market. Her hard work was evidenced in the *egusi* and *ogbonna* soups that were in bowls on her island. She turned on the vents and opened the kitchen window. Ejike would be back from Nnamdi's house any minute. He loved her cooking, but couldn't stand the smell of preparation.

Amara stepped into the living room just in time to answer her ringing phone. She smiled when the name "Chinelo" appeared on the caller ID.

"Hey, cuz. How are ya?" Amara used her free hand to turn on the ceiling fan.

"I *dey* o, my dear. What are you up to this lovely Saturday?" Chinelo asked.

"Nothing much. I just finished cooking."

"Ha, you and this cooking. That's why our time living together was so good. You loved to cook and I loved to eat."

Amara laughed. Those were the good old days. Straight out of college, living a carefree life. Her and Ejike, Chinelo and Udo or Afam—or whoever Chinelo was dealing with at the time. Her cousin had never been one to get too serious about any man. Amara grinned at the memory. She wouldn't change that time for the world except for that one month period when she was silly enough to break off the wedding and travel to Enugu to grieve her inability to have a child. Her mother finally talked sense into her and she returned. Luckily, Ejike took her back. She'd never forget how Chinelo had taken care of Ejike for her. If not for Chinelo's friendship with Ejike and her encouraging them to get back together, they wouldn't be married today.

"Where is Ejike?" Chinelo's question interrupted her thoughts.

"He coaches soccer every other Saturday. He should be at Nnamdi's by now."

"Ah, that one *sef*. How is Nnamdi? I saw his sister at the airport on my way here."

"Nnamdi's good, but has decided to remain a bachelor. I'm actively looking for a wife for him."

"Why? So he can leave your husband alone... *eben*?" Chinelo's laughter was so infectious that Amara had no choice but to join in.

"Yes, now *haba*." Amara paused. She suddenly had an idea. "Are you doing anything today?"

"No, I'm just watching TV now. Obinna went out with his uncle."

"I need to meet your son, oh. And tell him to ask his mother why I'm not his godmother," Amara said with a chuckle. "You want to come over for lunch? We have to catch up."

"How far is your house from Groton Circle? I'm not ready for all this *obodo yibo* traffic." Chinelo said.

Amara laughed at Chinelo's Igbo reference to "abroad."

"It's not far at all." Amara spent the next few minutes giving Chinelo detailed directions and the address for the taxi driver.

A short time later, a refreshed Amara stepped out of the shower for the second time that day. She put on a pair of white capris and a turquoise, one-sleeved blouse. She wrapped her hair in a loose bun on top of her head, allowing a few loose strands to fall. She looked in the mirror to apply lip gloss and some powder to her skinny face and noticed her breasts seemed to be getting larger. She pressed on them. They hurt a little.

It had been three weeks since her IVF, and she was trying to be calm. She didn't want to take a home pregnancy test because of the false positives she had gotten before. Her apprehension caused her to remain silent. She heard a whisper through the air, "Be anxious for nothing."

Amara knew it had to be God. She placed her hand on her stomach. It was flatter than a washboard. She prayed, "God, I claim that the seed of a child has been planted in the spiritual. I'm thanking you in advance for its manifestation in the natural. Amen."

She stuck out her stomach, imagining what she would look like pregnant. She wondered if she would have that glow. She rubbed her hands together in prayer and left the room.

Amara glanced at the clock that hung on the wall. Ejike was staying out longer than usual today. She wondered what he and Nnamdi had to talk about. She didn't want to disturb their guy bonding time, but Chinelo was coming over and Amara thought it would be a good idea for them to have lunch together and catch up on old times.

The doorbell chimed. She strode to the door as quickly as her legs could carry her and swung it open, screaming for joy when she came face to face with Chinelo. Chinelo squealed, too, as she stepped into the house. They hugged each other.

"Oh my God! You haven't changed a bit." Amara admired her cousin. She looked like the years or the fact that she'd had a baby didn't have any effect on her. The only thing that had changed was her hairstyle. She had traded her long mane for a natural, short haircut. People always referred to them as tea and coffee because of the contrast in their physical appearance.

"Chi, you look good."

"Look who's talking. You look fantastic." Chinelo made her way into the living area. "This house is nice."

Amara looked around the living room as if this was her first time seeing it. For her, sometimes it did seem surreal. It was hard spending her teen years in a village cut off from most of civilization. Their accommodations there were substandard compared to their home in Enugu. But the luxury of living in Enugu was snatched away for a couple of years when her dad got tired of waiting for her mother to conceive a second child. Like her grandfather, her dad thought polygamy was the answer to having another child. So he had relegated Amara and her mother to the village so his new wife could feel comfortable. When his new wife didn't conceive after two years, he moved them all back to Enugu. Those years were etched securely in Amara's memory. So any time she sat in her living room, she sent up a prayer of thanksgiving.

The wide space had a high ceiling and large windows that offered a good view of the front lawn. The light colored furniture set contrasted perfectly with the pumpkin brown walls that were covered in pictures of Amara and Ejike. The 52-inch flat screen television was Ejike's addition to the space. It was inserted in the nook above the mantel with an artificial wood-burning fireplace below.

"My dear, we thank God, oh." Amara offered Chinelo a seat. "Sit, sit, we have a lot of *gist* ground to cover."

Chinelo laughed. "You've always been a *gist* mistress. Where's your *bobo*?"

"Ejike's not back, but will soon be." Amara sat next to her cousin and crossed her legs. This was a good sign. At least Chinelo was asking of Ejike and not trying to change the subject when his name was mentioned.

They spent the next half hour talking and laughing, and reminiscing about the past and the present.

"*Ha na wa o*. So do you still keep in contact with Afam *sha*? At least for his son's sake?" Amara asked.

She couldn't believe Afam and Chinelo had gotten divorced. But then again their marriage was surprising, considering Chinelo was never deeply in love with him. Amara noticed Chinelo's hesitation in talking about the reason for her divorce. She decided to let the topic lie, but would continue to pray for her cousin. When Chinelo was ready to talk, she planned on being there to listen.

Amara stood and headed toward the kitchen. She heard the roar of the garage door opening. "Ejike is back. You two get reacquainted. Let me set the table."

A few moments later, Amara came out of the kitchen and stopped dead in her tracks. What she thought would be a nice surprise apparently wasn't. Ejike was standing there looking at Chinelo with a frozen fake smile. *What did this woman do to this man?*

"Hey, honey. How was practice?" Amara asked.

"Fine." Ejike walked over to Chinelo. "Hi, stranger. Long time."

"I know. She just disappeared." Amara said. "Well, I'm glad she decided to visit Dallas. I've told her that we have to meet her son as well."

"Yes, we do," Ejike said. Amara noticed the iciness in his voice

"Hi, yourself. I know. It's been ages. How've you been?" Chinelo stood and hugged him.

"We're good. Can't complain." Ejike turned around and reached for Amara.

She walked into his waiting arms. "I lured Chi over here to have lunch with us. Go and have a shower. Lunch is ready." Amara swatted Ejike's behind.

"Ouch, woman. You're going to pay for that."

"Really now?" Amara asked.

"Hmmm...*una go love oh. Abeg,* let me go first before you start your love games," Chinelo said.

"The love is sweet. What can I say?" Amara regretted the words the minute they came out of her mouth. She must have sounded so insensitive to Chinelo's situation. "I'm sorry—"

"Being divorced doesn't mean I can't be around people in love. Besides, I'll soon get what's mine." Chinelo smiled and headed to the table.

Amara had a puzzled look on her face as she followed Chinelo to the dining area. She could have sworn that she saw a bit of mischief in Chinelo's eyes.

CHAPTER 6

"Did you have to be so cold?" Amara asked Ejike as they prepared for church the following morning.

She turned her back to him. "Please, zip this up."

Ejike zipped up his wife's multi-colored, floral dress. "I don't know what you're talking about."

He looked in the mirror and looped one end of his tie around the other. This was one topic that Amara would not let rest. That was one of her major faults. She was too nice. Ejike didn't think there was anything wrong with being nice. After all, it was the Christian thing to do. But the Bible also said, "Be wise as a serpent." Amara always took people at face value, while he didn't. Since that wretched night, he decided he would never do that again.

Growing up in a polygamous household, Ejike learned early that you have to stay alert at all times. His dad's second wife was cunning and manipulative and caused his mother a lot of grief because she was always quick to come up with schemes and lies. That's why he'd never forgive himself for letting his guard down with Chinelo. He should have known better. Until he was sure that the Chinelo he saw yesterday was not the same person she was six years ago, all bets were off. He'd made that mistake once, but not again.

As he went into their walk-in closet, Ejike's thoughts traveled back to the month after Amara called off the wedding. He had just four weeks to make her see reason, but he was getting nowhere.

THE HARMATTAN BREEZE was blowing outside – perfect cuddle weather, but Amara was still camped out at her parent's house in Enugu. He had stopped by Swings and Shacks, the bar that had become the place to drown his sorrows. After a couple of drinks, he knew he was in no condition to drive home. He dialed Nnamdi, but there was no answer. The next number he dialed turned out to be the nail in his coffin.

Chinelo walked into the bar a few minutes later. She had taken a taxi so she'd be able to drive him home. The next thing he knew, they were in the apartment she shared with Amara.

Feeling drained, he didn't protest when she led him to the couch. He dragged her down with him. There was something familiar about the way her perfume teased his nostrils. It was the same fragrance Amara wore.

Chinelo kissed him on his forehead and stood. "Let me get you some coffee. You're going to have a humongous headache in the morning."

Within minutes, Chinelo had a cup of coffee set before him. The steam and aroma of the beverage made him sit up.

Chinelo sat next to him and rubbed his back while he sipped the drink slowly. That should have been his cue to leave. His body felt like it was being held down by some force of gravity.

"Please, don't worry about Amara. She'll come around. Let me know if you want seconds," she said.

He sighed. "Thank you." His head was spinning.

"My pleasure." She leaned over and touched a spot beside his mouth. "You had something there."

"Oh." Uncomfortable with the closeness, he reached for the napkin and wiped his mouth. "Is it good now?"

"No." Chinelo took the napkin from him. He could smell that perfume again as her face came within inches of his own. She slowly dabbed at the corner of his lips. "Now, that's better."

Ejike swallowed hard. There was something about the way Chinelo was looking at him.

That was his second cue to get out of there.

Reaching for his keys, he suddenly felt lightheaded. Ejike squeezed his eyes shut for a second. He thought he should have sobered up some by now. He should never have gone to that bar.

"Is everything okay?" Chinelo asked.

His head felt heavy as he nodded. He wanted to empty the contents of his stomach. Confused, he tried to stand up, only to fall back.

Chinelo got up and stood behind him. "Rest a little. At least finish your coffee." She rubbed his shoulders.

The warmth from her fingers made him feel even more disoriented. "I need to go," he slurred. "I'll call a taxi from here."

Chinelo's fingers moved to the side of his neck. "You sound really tired," she said. "I think you should rest for some time so you don't fall asleep in the taxi and end up someplace else."

What she said made sense. Chinelo wrapped an arm around his waist after he managed to pull himself up. She led the way to the bedroom.

He shook his head. He wasn't going to rest in her bedroom. "I'll stay here. On the couch, he said.

"Hush now, you need to be able to stretch out. Don't worry. We're going to your Amara's room." Chinelo pushed open the bedroom door with her foot.

Even though something kept telling him he needed to leave, he gave a sigh of relief as he stretched out on the bed.

Chinelo leaned over and loosened his tie. "Maybe you should take off your shirt so it doesn't get rumpled," she said.

When his shaky fingers couldn't work the buttons, Chinelo sat next to him on the bed. Within minutes, both his shirt and trousers were off. He didn't ask for his trousers to be taken off.

The out of body sensations running through him made it difficult for him to think. "Chi...what's ...go...going on?"

She lay beside him. "I just want you to be more comfortable." She began rubbing a hand on his chest.

He knew it wasn't right, but he had no fight left. He tried to move, but his legs felt like lead poles.

Chinelo's warm breath fanned his ear. "Just relax."

His eyes began to flutter and soon everything around him faded to black.

The blare of the early morning Muslim call to prayer woke Ejike up. Looking at the light purple walls, it took him sometime to realize where he was.

The light snoring beside him made him turn. Looking at Chinelo's peaceful face, a sense of dread welled up inside him. No! What had he done?

Shaking, he lifted up the duvet and saw that they were both naked, the way God had created them. Ejike's mouth filled with bile.

EJIKE'S MEMORY took a detour back to the present when he heard Amara's voice. "Honey, are you listening to me?" Amara entered the closet. She was fiddling with her bracelet as she walked over to her shoe area.

"Huh? What did you say?"

"Don't play coy. I just don't understand. You guys were friends," Amara slipped her well-manicured feet into her pumps.

"Babe, there's a season for everything. She was my friend then, but only because we were course mates. Then we continued because she's your cousin. That season has passed. Besides, what's the big deal anyway?" Ejike walked back into the bedroom. He didn't absolve himself of any part of their unholy rendezvous, but Chinelo had deliberately taken advantage of his vulnerability. She was sober, he was not.

He shook his head in disgust as he remembered the wink and light touches Chinelo gave him when Amara wasn't looking at lunch the day before. She was up to something and it couldn't be good.

Amara walked over to him and began straightening his tie. Ejike stared down at his wife.

She met his gaze and shrugged. "Nothing really, I guess." She patted down his tie and walked to the bed to get her clutch and hand him the keys. "Well, please be nice. She's coming to stay with us next weekend." She opened the bedroom door and walked out.

Ejike hurriedly followed her. "She's coming to where?" He probably didn't hear correctly the first time.

"Here," Amara said. "Her son will be going to Austin with his other cousins. She'll stay with us for two days.

"When did this happen?"

"Come on, honey. It's Chinelo. Did I need to take permission?"

Ejike wanted to shout, "yes" but that would give Amara a reason to be suspicious and question him more. Right there and then he decided that he would busy himself with work as much as possible. It was just two days. No weapon formed against him shall prosper. He could do this.

"No, you didn't. A heads up would've been nice. But it's all good." He smiled. "Let's get going."

WHEN AMARA and Ejike entered The Way Living Church, the praise team had already started singing. Ejike looked around. The sanctuary was kind of full this morning. Ejike loved the praise and worship part of the service, especially the way they alternated between slow and fast songs.

Their usual seats were still empty. Excusing themselves, they eased into the pew. Amara set her clutch and Bible down and started dancing to the beat. Ejike admired his wife. She was his virtuous woman.

"Hey, y'all. Man, scoot over." Ejike looked around to see David Walker and his wife Tonye. They all sat together every once in a while. Ejike assumed that since the sanctuary was fuller than normal, the Walker's regular seat had been taken.

"Hey, man. How's it going?" Ejike shook David's outstretched hand and then kissed Tonye's cheek.

"Good, man. We're running late," David said.

"We just got here ourselves. I wonder why the church is so packed. Not that I'm complaining. We need to draw more people into the kingdom," Ejike said.

Amara and Tonye exchanged pleasantries and they all got back to worshipping.

A short while later, after the announcements had been made, Pastor Harris walked up to the podium. He looked like he just stepped out of the K& G Men's Warehouse store. He had on a three-piece, ash colored suit with a lime green shirt.

"Praise the Lord, everybody." The man of God took off his jacket and handed it to his assistant. He dabbed his forehead with a white towel and said, "I say, praise the Lord, everybody."

Shouts, of "Hallelujah" and "Amen" came from the crowd. Satisfied, Pastor Harris bowed his head and said a short prayer. "And let the church say—"

A thunderous, "Amen" came from the congregation.

"We are going to get real and serious today. Turn to Ephesians 4, and let's read verses 24 to 25."

The congregation recited the verses in unison. *"And to put on the new self, created to be like God in true righteousness and holiness.*

Therefore, having put away falsehood, let each one of you speak the truth with his neighbor, for we are members one of another."

Ejike shifted in his seat and looked around. *Someone must be pranking me.* Why did the pastor have to preach from this verse today, of all the days of the year?

"Our focus today is on how we're going to get our God to say, 'Well done' when we get to those pearly gates. After your sojourn here on earth, will He tell you, 'Well done, my child?' First of all, you know that you have to accept and believe in Christ as your Lord and Savior. But after that, then what?" he asked and looked around.

He continued, "Most Christians think that once they're born again, they have reached the finish line. But that's far from the truth. That's when the race is just starting. We need to do those things that God has sent us to do while keeping our eye on the prize, which is being one with Christ. How do we do that in our daily lives?

"We are sinners and have come short of His glory. It's only by the grace of God, but we shouldn't take that grace for granted. Every day, let's conduct ourselves in a way that when those who haven't come to Christ see you, they will want to know your God. Remember people see how you act before they hear what you say.

"Let us wake up every day with the resolve of getting better at conquering those vices which plague us. Like falsehood. Are you being deceitful? Do you have anger issues, harshness, lying, and corrupt speech? Don't give the devil a foothold in your life. Because as you know, once you open the door, he will come in and relax."

At the end of the message, some people stood up and clapped, while others shouted, "You better preach it, Pastor."

Ejike could do neither. A chilling sensation came over him. For the past six years, he had lived in falsehood and deceitfulness. Chinelo's reappearance in Dallas after all this time had to be his punishment.

Chapter 7

The weather outside could only be described with one word. Gorgeous. It was sunny with clear, blue skies and a light breeze. Chinelo's brother, Gozie, took Obinna and his kids to the park. They did everything but grovel for her to go with them, but she knew she wouldn't be any fun.

Chinelo absently stared at the television. She couldn't find anything to hold her attention. As matter of fact, nothing held her interest lately. Not since she got back from Amara's house some days ago.

Chinelo tossed the remote control on the sofa and went into the kitchen. She reached for a glass from the top cabinet and opened the refrigerator for some sweet tea. After taking a sip of the beverage, she smacked her lips at its sweetness. It was though they emptied all the sugar in China into this tea. She took another gulp, leaned against the island, and stared out the window waiting for the rice she had on the stove to come to a boil.

The past six years of her life flashed before her. How did she get so unlucky in the love department? She had endured years of unrequited love from Ejike—hoping and dreaming that one day, he would see the light and give them a chance. When Ejike began to take an interest in Amara, Chinelo still didn't believe it was over for her until she saw the engagement ring. But her heart refused to reconcile what her eyes saw, even with all the pre-wedding preparations going on.

Her chance to give it one last try came when Amara, in her "martyr" attitude, had broken off the engagement and run to Enugu. Spoiled brat. Amara's whole attitude made Chinelo so mad. Amara had succeeded in taking the man that should have been hers, yet she couldn't see past her issue that Ejike didn't seem to care about. So she didn't deserve him.

The bubbling noise from the stove meant the rice was ready to be washed a second time. She was cooking coconut rice, the same meal she was cooking when she got Ejike's call that fateful night. It couldn't have played out any better if she had planned it herself. It was a good thing she was home. That night was fabulous. Everything she had imagined it would be. All those years of waiting was so worth it. The way he came alive in her arms told her that Amara had been holding out on the man. Chinelo was sure that after that performance, he would see just what he was missing. But she was not prepared for the aftermath.

"WHAT IN THE WORLD? Are you crazy?" Ejike barked, jumping out of the bed.

Chinelo eased up to a sitting position. She rubbed her eyes and stretched her body. Memories of the night before came flooding back. She smiled. "Good Morning,"

He wasn't barking last night oh, but let me hold my tongue like a church girl. Amara always says a soft answer turns away wrath or something like that.

"What's so good about the morning? What have we done?" He pulled on his clothes.

"You were tired, so I wanted you to relax."

"Oh my God! I'm finished." He searched around for something.

"If you are looking for your wallet and keys, they're in the living room." She got up from the bed and put on her robe. She caught up with him just as he was about to open the door. She inhaled his smell. A very manly man.

"Ejike, hold on. You must feel what I feel. I've been in love with you since before Amara came along. And see what she has done." She raised her hand to rub his face. He grabbed her hand before it made contact. His grip around her wrist hurt.

"You're sick. Do you realize you're talking about your cousin? Amara looks up to you as a big sister." He flung her hand away and put both of his hands over his head. "I am finished."

"Calm down. Just think about it. I can be so much more than Amara can be for you. Besides, I'm fertile."

The change in the color of his face told her that was probably the wrong thing to say. The heat rising up in his body seeped out. She felt his anger. He walked towards her. She moved back.

"Don't you ever imply that Amara is infertile again. And a word of this to her and I will kill you." He opened the door and stormed out. A few seconds later, another slam of the front door told her that he had left. Chinelo didn't see him again until the wedding three weeks later.

In the days following their unholy rendezvous, with Afam on a business trip to Ghana, Ejike's cousin, Udo, had been her solace and shoulder to cry on. One night, one thing led to another and she found herself being intimate with yet another Dike. He and Ejike shared the same blood and looked almost identical, but it wasn't the same thing. She and Udo both agreed that they made a mistake sleeping together. They didn't want to ruin their friendship.

In the ensuing weeks, Udo thought her continuous tears were because he was leaving for Germany in a few weeks. However, her tears were because of the pregnancy test she took. Resigning herself to fate, she accepted the marriage proposal Afam had on the table for several months.

Chinelo placed the pot back on the stove with more force than intended. Why did some people have to have more luck than others? Amara always got the admirers to fall head over heels for her. Chinelo always had to go the extra mile for attention. She spent serious Naira on the latest clothes, shoes, her hair, and nails. Even after six years of a childless marriage, Amara still had Ejike eating out of her hands.

The phone rang. She went in search of it in the living room and located it on the sofa. The caller ID indicated that it was a United Kingdom number. She answered the call.

"Hello," Chinelo said.

"Hello, Chi. It's me, Ijeoma."

Chinelo looked at the caller ID again. "Ij, what are you doing in the UK?"

"My husband's company was sponsoring him for a two-week conference, so I decided to tag along," Ijeoma said. "How is Obi? Have you guys seen the doctors yet?"

"Yes, we have. And he's doing well. He went out with my brother and his kids." Chinelo was so happy to hear Ijeoma's voice. She really missed her friend.

Soon after she and Afam got married in a small court wedding, he was transferred to Abuja. That's where she had met Ijeoma. Ijeoma was married to a very successful architect and had her own boutique in the Maitama area of Abuja. Since Chinelo always pursued the latest fashions, it didn't take long for her to locate the new boutique. She became a regular and their friendship quickly evolved into a sisterhood. But with limits. Chinelo loved everything about Ijeoma, but when she started calling Jesus in every statement, that's where Chinelo drew the line.

The Jesus Ijeoma kept calling hadn't been so good to her.

Where was He when her parents died when she was eight, leaving just her and brother? Where was He when she had gone through all the trials and tribulations of the past years? A lost love, a sick son, a broken marriage. He always seemed to answer other people prayers and not hers. So no, she didn't really want to hear about Jesus.

"When will he get the transplant?"

"We have an appointment in a couple of weeks to talk about donor options. After that we should be good to go," Chinelo replied.

"Praise God. How long after that will you come home?" Ijeoma asked.

Chinelo didn't answer her.

"Chi, when are you coming home?"

"Umm, don't know yet. It's kind of nice here—"

"Chinelo, what do you mean?"

"Nothing, just that it's nice here." Chinelo wedged the phone between her shoulder and ear. She uncrossed her legs and reached for the Jet magazine on the center table. She absently skimmed through the pages as she continued to talk to her friend. They laughed and chatted a few more minutes, and then hung up.

Chinelo wasn't about to tell Ijeoma that if things went according to plan, she was thinking of making herself a home in the United States. When she boarded a flight to Dallas some weeks ago, she had one thing on her mind. To get her son proper medical attention and in the process, get what was hers. So she didn't need any lectures or quotes from the Bible. Not now.

Step one, her weekend stay with the Dikes. This weekend, she would remind Ejike about what they had that night. What they could have now. She would no longer be denied his love. If he didn't come willingly, he would come by force. Either way, she was going to get what should have been hers all along.

CHAPTER 8

The week had gone by in a blur and another Friday was here at last. But this one was special. Amara went around the room again to make sure everything was in place. She fluffed the already fluffed pillow for the umpteenth time. Chinelo should be here any minute and she wanted everything to go perfectly. It'd just be like old times. She had finally convinced Ejike to behave and she trusted her husband to keep his word.

She walked into the kitchen and checked the fish in the oven. It had baked perfectly. Amara snickered when remembered Ejike's warning about not stressing herself out.

"If she doesn't like it here, she can always go back to her brother's house," Ejike had said when he left in the morning.

The doorbell chimed. Amara hurriedly made her way to the door. On the other side of it stood a smiling Chinelo.

"Hey, sis," Amara stepped aside for Chinelo to gain entry. "I'm so glad you're here, even if it's just for a couple of days.

"Not as happy as I am." Chinelo put her overnight bag down and reached out to give Amara a brief hug.

"Let's get your stuff to the room. It's the weekend, baby!"

Amara moved her body from side to side in a dance, making her way to the staircase.

Some minutes later, after Chinelo was all settled in, they made their way to the kitchen.

"How is Obinna? I know he was sad to see you go." Amara turned on the oven to heat the fish up. She glanced at her watch. Ejike had promised to make it back in time so they wouldn't be late for the concert.

"My dear, he didn't even notice I was leaving." Chinelo picked up some glasses and silverware and made her way to the table. "He's having too much fun."

"I'm glad *jare*. That's what the summer is supposed to be about." Amara paused and wondered whether she should bring up his doctor's appointment. The last time Chinelo had talked about her son's ailment, it took a while to bring her out of the funk she got in. Although Amara had prayed with Chinelo, she had a feeling that Chinelo didn't have faith that God could heal the boy. She was more inclined to believe the statistics of the mortality rate of someone with a high-risk case like Obinna's. Amara tried to tell her of God's healing power. The doctors would do their bit, but God would finish it up.

Amara continued to pray, only imagining what Chinelo must be going through. She decided to ask anyway. "When do you take him to the doctor next?"

"We haven't had any problems since we got here. Maybe America is what he needs." Chinelo laughed, probably at Amara's expression. "I'm joking oh, before you start preaching. You know it's not hard for you to whip out a sermon." Chinelo walked out of the kitchen to the dining room.

"Preach about what? I was just surprised you'd even consider it. You love Nigeria.'" Amara was puzzled by Chinelo's tone and defensiveness, but decided to ignore it.

"Yeah, right. Anyway, did I tell you the other day that I really like what you've done with this place?" Chinelo asked.

"Yes, and thanks," Amara shouted from the kitchen. She loved to decorate and was already envisioning how she would turn the guest room into a nursery. She was thinking about the results she would get soon in a positive light. This time, she would speak and think her baby into existence.

The two women worked in semi-silence, setting the table and laying out the spread of grilled fish and rice pilaf with veggies. Chinelo was pouring water into the glasses when Amara's phone rang.

"Phone call," Chinelo shouted to Amara who had entered the restroom.

It was probably Ejike. He promised to be home early for the concert. Amara quickly put herself back together, washed her hands and exited the bathroom.

Amara picked up her phone from the mantle and looked at the caller ID. It wasn't Ejike, but one of her clients. Darius Brooks was the manager of an athlete who couldn't seem to stay on the right path. Before she answered the call, she knew it was trouble.

With disappointment in her voice, she answered the phone. "Hey Darius, don't tell me Tray got in trouble again. That's the only reason you could be calling me at this time on a Friday afternoon." Amara's eyebrow rose, and then scrunched in anger as she listened to Darius tell her about Tray's recent woes.

"I can't make it now. I have a guest." She paused and turned to see Chinelo watching her. Amara listened to Darius give her a million and one reasons why it wasn't Tray's fault this time. After a few more minutes, the muscles in Amara's face began to relax.

"Okay, but I won't stay for the entire news conference. Like I told you, I have a house guest and we have plans." Amara sighed, then continued, "It's about time you put that client of yours in check. Just as the club hired him, they can also fire him." Amara hung up the phone.

"Is everything okay? This PR work is very demanding," Chinelo said.

Amara ran her fingers through her hair. "I've got to go down-town for a while. I'll be gone for about an hour, max."

"Is everything okay?" Chinelo asked again.

"There is this client of mine that manages an athlete who is too juvenile for his own good. He has a sense of entitlement that makes him do crazy things." Amara rammed her hands between the cushions of the couch in search of her keys.

"What do they want from you?"

"The boy has gotten himself in some trouble and I have to coach him for an impromptu news conference his team owners want to have."

"What about lunch?

"I'll soon be back, but if Ejike gets home before I do, you guys can go ahead." Amara raced up the stairs to change.

THIS WAS WORKING out better than Chinelo thought. Amara had been gone for a little over half an hour. She had tried calling Ejike before she left, but couldn't get to him. Chinelo smiled because that meant Ejike had no idea that he'd be coming home to her.

As soon as Amara left the house, Chinelo took a quick shower and put on her blue jean mini skirt and a sheer, white blouse. Despite the black tank top underneath, it still had the effect she was going for.

Moments later, she could hear the garage door opening. *That must be Ejike. Amara couldn't have made it back so soon.*

Chinelo adjusted the twins on her chest. Even if God hadn't done anything else, He had endowed her with a good cup size and a figure she could always count on. She hiked up her skirt a little and sat on the sofa.

"Showtime, phase one," Chinelo whispered under her breath.

The adjoining door to the garage opened. Chinelo snickered

when Ejike stopped dead in his tracks. He blinked a few times, then regained his composure. She felt the emotion in his eyes as he made a quick sweep of her body. Scorn. Discomfort. But she noticed that didn't stop him from staring at her legs a second longer. That was what Chinelo had counted on—she knew he was a leg man. She remembered it was Amara's legs he salivated over first. It was nice to know that being a church man hadn't affected his sight. Chinelo did a sweep of her own. Now that Amara wasn't home, there was no need to steal glances like she had done at lunch the other day.

Ejike Dike was still the most beautiful man she had ever seen. His neatly cut hair and lean but toned frame could be lethal on any sane woman's hormones. His dark eyes always seemed to have the ability to see right through someone. Chinelo also noticed his style hadn't been affected by the years either. He had on dark blue khakis and a Tommy Hilfiger, multi-colored T-shirt that hugged his muscles like it was made especially for him. Chinelo stood up and reached out to grab his portfolio and the bottle of wine he brought home.

"Where is Amara?" Ejike walked past her and scanned the room with his eyes.

Chinelo felt her blood rise. He just walked by her as though she didn't exist. She couldn't lose her head though. She was on a mission. *This man hasn't seen anything yet.*

"Well, hello to you, too," Chinelo said.

"Hi, where is Amara?"

"You trust your wife now. She's always trying to rescue people. She had to run out for a bit to meet with a client." Chinelo made an attempt to reach for his portfolio again. This time he let her have it. She walked to the staircase and set it down at the foot of the stairs. She would have taken it into the study, but this time they had was valuable before his goody two shoes wife returned. She was not about to leave him alone. Every moment was precious.

"Why didn't she call me?" Ejike asked.

Chinelo could tell he was distracted. "She tried—"

"Urgh... I guess it was when my phone died. I couldn't charge it since I left my car charger at home," Ejike said.

"She'll soon be back. Lunch is ready. Come, let me serve you. Amara said to go ahead without her." Chinelo headed towards the dining table, but noticed that Ejike was not following her.

"Why are you standing there?"

"Chinelo, the last time I put what you brought me in my mouth, I ended up in your bed. I'm still not sure you didn't put anything in that coffee."

"What are you implying? In your subconscious, you wanted all this." She ran her hands down her hips and twirled around. "That's why you ended up in my bed."

"What do you really want?" Ejike asked.

Chinelo scoffed and clapped her hands together softly, as though she was dusting them off. "What kind of question is that?" She laughed, walking toward him. "I'm your in-law, oh."

"Oh, so you know that?"

"*Abeg* get off your high horse. Don't even dare put it all on me." She removed a non-existent piece of lint from his shoulder.

He caught her hand. "You took advantage of my drunkenness."

"I take exception to that. I wanted you to relax. How was I to know that you'd want to get frisky?" She giggled. "I was just a willing participant."

His fist balled. "Chinelo, listen to me carefully. Whatever evil you're planning is not going to work. If that's why you're dressed like that, then you've grossly miscalculated."

"Ha, I'm glad you noticed. I thought you were immune." She smiled.

"I am immune. Back then, I let my guard down because I thought you were someone I could trust. But I know better and I'll not let you hurt Amara," Ejike said. He walked back to the living room, taking off his jacket and loosening his tie.

"Ejike, I'm tired of your self-righteous cry. You and I had sex. End of story. Whether you were drunk or not isn't the point. You enjoyed it and so did I," Chinelo said, following him.

Chinelo paused. From his face, he clearly wanted to strangle her, but she was not going to let his hostility faze her.

"Don't you see we just did what we should have done a long time ago before Amara entered the picture? I should be the one here. She took you from me," she said, referring to the house. "And still, she hasn't been able to do what other women can." She paused to read his expression. It was blank. She continued, "A child, Ejike. You are an only son. Who would succeed you?"

Ejike's jaw tightened. Chinelo thought a vein would pop on the side of his head. She knew she hit a sore spot. In silence, she waited for the aftermath.

"Chinelo, are you normal? You're sounding insane," Ejike said.

Chinelo laughed. "I'm as sane as I've ever been. You're the one acting mad. Are you sure Amara didn't give you love potion? I heard those things are really potent and last for years. Her *churchousness* might be a front?" Chinelo sneered. She was enjoying taunting him.

"I see you are having fun. Rather than have you hold this over me, I'll do what I should have done years ago—tell Amara." He stood and proceeded to the stairs.

"Oh, come on. You know you wouldn't. If you could, you'd have done so a long time ago." She crossed her legs at the knees and leaned back into the chair.

"You really think so?" Ejike asked with one foot on the stair.

"I know so. That wife of yours sees black and white. There is no middle ground for her. No matter how you want to spin it...you cheated," Chinelo said.

Ejike gave her a stern look, but she didn't back down. She was tired of him making this all her fault. After a few seconds, he retreated upstairs.

He can run, but he can't hide. Men are visual creatures. I'll just have to give him something to look at this weekend.

Ejike was going to be hers whether he liked it or not. She had a couple of tricks up her sleeve and trump card no one knew about. By the time she was done, Ejike was going to be a permanent fixture in her life.

Chapter 9

"Why are you up so early?" Amara tied a scarf on her head as she entered the kitchen.

"Good morning, sis," Chinelo said, barely glancing back. She scooped up the cooked batch of *akara*—a bean cake—from the oil and stirred the remainder of the bean puree used to make it. The oil popped.

Amara rushed to her side. "Good morning. Take it easy, *abeg*."

"Thank you *jare*. I'm okay."

"How was the concert?" Amara opened the refrigerator to get the juice.

"It was nice oh. Your husband was the complete gentleman." Chinelo moved swiftly to turn on the electric kettle for hot water. Ejike really wasn't, but there was no need for Amara to know that because she would take it upon herself to run interference. Chinelo didn't need her to work on Ejike. She would do it herself.

Last night, as lady luck would have it, Amara didn't return home in time for the concert. Regardless of what Ejike said about confessing to Amara, Chinelo knew he couldn't do it. He ended up taking her to the concert against his will. He must have done it so as not to raise Amara's suspicions. Whatever the case, it had worked in Chinelo's favor.

"Don't tell me you're making custard?" Amara asked excitedly. "That's Ejike's favorite breakfast."

Of course it is. Why do you think I'm making it? "Oh really? I didn't know that. I like it, too, so decided to treat you guys."

"*Daalu.* Thank you." Amara picked up a ball of *akara* and took a bite. "Have you called Obinna?"

"Yes, he's doing well. Can't wait for me to come home tomorrow," Chinelo said.

"You'll go to church with us first, *abi*?"

"Amara, you know I don't do all these church things."

"Come on, Chi. You can't still be like that. Jesus loves you and you have to know that."

Chinelo thought for a minute. *If He loved me, you wouldn't be in this house – I would. Why didn't He make that prayer come true? If He loved me I won't be here trying to get medical help for a son that I love with all my heart.*

But Chinelo was not in the mood to get Pastor Amara started. She had more important things on her mind. Like how to get Ejike to stop ignoring her. Last night, he had been like a robot. He only talked to her when she asked something. If only he would lighten up, he would see that she had so much more to offer than Amara did.

Chinelo smiled, "Okay I'll go. Before you step up on the podium and start preaching." The ladies laughed.

After a few minutes, Chinelo said, "Everything is all set. Let me run up and take a shower. I don't want to smell like beans all day."

"Ejike should be down as well. He has a meeting at the church," Amara said.

"Church *ke*? I thought he would be going sightseeing with us." Chinelo asked, one foot on the steps. The minute she said the words, she wish she hadn't. Even to her ears, she sounded too eager. She didn't want Amara to suspect her intentions. Her cousin could be pretty naive, so there really was a fat chance of that happening.

"Yes, church. We have a retreat coming up that he's planning. *Oya,* go and shower. We have a lot to see today."

Minutes later, Chinelo listened through the guest bedroom door. She had showered and lotioned her body, but deliberately didn't put on her clothes. With her towel loosely tucked between her breasts, she opened her door at the exact moment she heard Ejike open his.

They came face to face with each other and Chinelo let her towel slip a couple of inches down her chest. She saw the look on Ejike's face as he willed himself to turn away.

"Oops, I'm sorry. Good morning." She pulled her towel up and secured it around her chest. She noticed that Ejike hadn't said a word. Instead, the intensity she thought she saw in his eyes a minute ago had changed to disgust.

"Good morning," he said, barely audible. He brushed past her and made his way down the stairs.

This man fine sha.

Ejike looked especially handsome in his green and blue, Ralph Lauren T-shirt with knee-length, khaki shorts. He looked like one of the models in the Old Navy commercials she had been seeing since she got here. She was sure that the leather moccasins he used to round off his look were custom made. She hadn't seen that kind before.

She would let him play hard to get for now, if that was the way he wanted to go. But she wouldn't put up with it for much longer. After all, she knew she had something he wanted.

CHINELO SLAMMED the hair pick down on the dresser. The weekend had virtually gone by without a dent being made in

Ejike's attitude towards her. She had apologized for the towel incident right before he left for his church the previous morning. She made sure Amara was out of sight when she went up to him to apologize. She didn't mean the apology, but if that's what he wanted, she'd oblige. Anything to make him smile at her.

Chinelo was fully aware that he only acknowledged her because of Amara and it made her blood boil.

After he left, she and Amara had spent virtually the whole day in one store after the other. Chinelo had to admit that she'd had fun. But, she didn't want to let all the emotion for Amara cloud her mission. To get through the day, Chinelo had to keep reminding herself that all was fair in love and war.

Chinelo sometimes wondered how Amara could be so naive that she almost felt sorry for her. Amara was acting like she wasn't born and raised in Nigeria. How could she let another woman come into her home and encourage her to go out with her husband? Family or not, Chinelo could never allow herself to be so naive. She didn't trust other women and she had no idea how Amara did, especially since she was childless. Chinelo knew that if she were the one, she'd be paranoid about every woman her husband talked to. Amara was too trusting. Well that attitude just might cost her. Chinelo pushed the thought to the back of her mind. She had to focus.

Now she had to prepare to go to church. That was the last place she wanted to be. She wanted to go home and work on the second phase of her plot since the first one seemed to be failing.

Chinelo inspected her face for the last time in the bathroom mirror. She could hear Amara screaming from downstairs that they were about to be late. These were the things that she just didn't understand. Amara had been praying to her Jesus for six years now and He hadn't given her a child, yet she was so joyful that it was almost pathetic.

Chinelo refreshed her lipstick and nodded at the way her lilac dress hugged her hips. She picked up her overnight bag and exited the room.

~

Chinelo followed as Ejike and Amara strolled hand in hand into The Way Living Church. Their public display of affection was sickening. Ejike was probably putting on a show for her benefit. She was sure they didn't walk that way all the time. They had been married for a while now.

Chinelo watched as they greeted a couple of people and introduced her before they settled down in a pew closer to the front than she would have liked. The church seemed like it had been newly renovated or they had a top-notch maintenance crew. Amara said they had been going here since they moved to the U.S, so she concluded that the church had to be old.

Chinelo followed Amara's lead and swayed to the beat of the song the choir sang.

"I simply love this church. They have songs that speak to you. And the pastor's message always hits a nerve," Amara whispered into Chinelo's ear so she could hear her above the music.

"Really? What is the church about? I mean apart from the Jesus part?" Chinelo asked. As far as she could remember, all the pastors ever wanted was money for whatever project they could come up with.

Amara smiled. "Besides the obvious, we also do a lot of outreach programs. Telling people of His love."

"Hmmm, okay," Chinelo said. She hoped Amara wouldn't go on and on. She already had to endure what their pastor, who had just stepped up to the podium, was about to say.

"That's Pastor Harris," Amara said.

"*Ehen*, I figured as much," Chinelo whispered back.

The worship songs died down and the pastor went straight into the sermon after a short prayer.

"Jesus doesn't care about what you've been, who you've been with, or how you got to the state you're in. All He cares about is the present. Where do you want to go? Where do you want to end up in eternity? Are you ready to acknowledge Him today? Your past doesn't matter. Turn with me to John 4:13-15: *Jesus answered, "Everyone who drinks this water will be thirsty again, but whoever drinks the water I give them will never thirst. Indeed, the water I give them will become in them a spring of water welling up to eternal life." The woman said to him, "Sir, give me this water so that I won't get thirsty and have to keep coming here to draw water.*

"You can't keep beating yourself up about things you did in the past that keep you running away from the only One that can give you a clean slate. Ain't nobody got time for all that self-pity. We have all sinned and come short of His glory, but the wonderful thing is that our God is a loving God. Don't get it twisted, though. He's also a consuming fire, but that's a whole different sermon."

The congregation laughed.

Chinelo shifted in her seat. This is why she didn't like this church business. They were always trying to make somebody feel bad about this salvation stuff. If Jesus was so good, then why did bad things happen to those that served him? She glanced at Amara. She was being so attentive, soaking in the pastor's every word. Chinelo looked at her watch. *This thing should be over soon.*

"Jesus knew He was breaking the rules by talking to the woman at the well. Then He even went a step further to ask her for something to drink. That is how Christ demonstrates His love. He is no respecter of persons and offers everyone salvation and a good life through Him, but you have to be willing to accept Him as your Lord and Savior. The woman at the well was ashamed of her ways and tired of hearing people talk about her. Y'all know you church folk are so judgmental."

Some people in the congregation shouted, "preach."

"But that doesn't move Jesus. He will accept you just as you are, but you must be willing to come. Like the Samaritan woman, in spite of your sins or past, you must be willing to drink of the living water. That's the only way to eternal life. It's your choice."

The ushers walked to the front and with outstretched arms, they beckoned for people to come forward and give their lives to Christ. Chinelo was glad Amara didn't look at her. If she had, she might have been forced to curse her out. Nicely, of course, since they were in a church. Chinelo turned and focused on Ejike. He was so much into this church thing that by herself, she wouldn't be able to break him. It was time to pull out her trump card.

CHAPTER 10

Ejike closed his office door. He had seen the last client off. His calendar was normally filled with back-to-back meetings on Tuesdays, but today had started off slow. He was glad it had picked up in the end with unexpected clients. That was a good thing since it took his mind off his worries. Worries Nnamdi called self-imposed were now very real. This past weekend with Chinelo in his house would definitely go down as the most miserable weekend of his married life.

Ejike stood and walked to the mini fridge in his office. He reached for a bottle of water, twisted the cap off, and took a sip. He walked over to the window. The stunning view of the city from the twenty-six story building in which his office was located always calmed his raging mind.

The last Sunday's sermon was on constant replay in his mind. If all the tugging the Holy Spirit was doing to his conscience wasn't enough, Chinelo's antics this past weekend were a sure enough sign that he needed to come clean now. In his head, he knew it, but his heart was scared of the aftermath. It would destroy Amara and subsequently him. He knew that he probably should take a chance and come clean, then rely on the grace of God to see him through. Grace. That should have provided comfort, but it didn't. Like Apostle Paul, his spirit was willing, but his flesh was weak. Right now, he feared that Chinelo might just be crazy enough to tell Amara everything and then some.

Ejike beamed when he remembered that today, they would hopefully be getting good news. Amara had a doctor's appointment that she insisted she wanted to go to by herself. He glanced at his watch and went back to his desk to gather up some files. His intention was to be home when she got back. Either way the results read, he wanted to be there for her.

A knock on the door interrupted what he was doing. He straightened his frame and folded his arms across his chest.

"Yes, come in." He really didn't need anything getting in the way of him going home.

"Hi, Ejike. There's a lady here to see you," Amanda, his assistant of the last three years said. She had started off as an intern, but quickly became very efficient at her job, so the firm asked her to come back once she graduated.

"Oh, why didn't you use the intercom?"

"I was up anyway. And I also wanted to bring these in." She placed the folder she was carrying on the table. "It's the file for today. Before I put it away, I need your signature in one more place."

"Oh, okay." He picked up a pen and signed on the line Amanda pointed to. "Are you ready to leave?" Ejike glanced up at her.

"Yes, once I send her in, I'll be on my way," Amanda said.

"Did she give a name?"

"Yes, Chinelo Edozie," Amanda announced casually.

For Ejike, however, the mention of that name felt like cold water had just been thrown on him. *What is she doing here? At this time? Without Amara?*

"Err… okay, send her in and you can leave. Good night."

Ejike hadn't had time to prepare himself when the door

opened and Chinelo walked in. Their eyes locked. In hers, he could recognize mischief. In his, he was sure there was despair.

She smiled. The same sinister smile she had worn all weekend.

"Are you just going to stand there?" Chinelo walked toward him with her arms outstretched.

He brushed her hands aside and walked past her to close the door. "What are you doing here?" Ejike walked to his desk and leaned against it.

Chinelo sat on the one of the chairs in the corner. "So what's been going on?"

"Since last weekend?" He paused. "Nothing much. Just working and trying to make a living."

The rise of her eyebrow convinced him that his hostility wasn't lost on her.

"Don't be that way,' Chinelo said with a smirk on her face. She uncrossed and crossed her legs again.

"Listen, I don't have time for this. State your mission or leave. I need to get home."

Chinelo was silent. Ejike could feel her intense stare. She did not answer his question. He really didn't want to hear her mission. He just wanted her to disappear.

"What are you doing here?"

"I just came over to talk." Chinelo said.

"About what?"

"Why you're still so bitter? It's been six years. Get over it." Chinelo flung her hand in the air dismissively.

Ejike paused for a few moments. The air of calmness surrounding her worried him the most. Her motive for visiting wasn't as clear cut as she wanted him to believe. Amara did say her son was sick. For someone who had that to worry about, she was too busy worrying about him.

"How long will you be in the US?"

Chinelo's eyebrows crunched up, forming a frown. "Are you chasing me away? What kind of question is that?"

"No type of question. I'm assuming you have a home and life to go back to. Or are you relocating?" By the time the question came out of his mouth, he regretted it. He didn't want to give her any ideas.

"Can't call it much of a home. As you know, I'm divorced. And now that you mention it, relocating wouldn't be such a bad idea."

Ejike decided to sidestep her last remark. "Yeah, Amara did mention you were divorced. Sorry to hear that." He studied her for a few seconds. Her expression was blank. "Irreconcilable differences?"

Just as she was about to answer, his phone buzzed on the table. He started to answer it, but decided to let it go to voicemail. He wanted to get this visit over with. The special ringtone assigned to his mailbox buzzed, so he knew the person had left a message. He turned to face Chinelo.

"You could say that. The chief bone of contention was my son," she said.

"Why?" Ejike asked. *No wonder she's here disturbing my life. Hers has fallen apart.*

"At birth, my son was diagnosed with a blood disease called Thalassemia. He has to be transfused quite often. His condition started taking a toll on the family. The cost and the effect mentally were too much. My marriage couldn't survive it."

Ejike felt compassion for her. "I don't understand why a man would push his wife and son out because of an ailment that's hereditary." He saw her shrink back.

Men who couldn't be the man God called them to be irritated him. Especially when there were children involved. Just like his dad. He couldn't seem to pull it together even if it was just for the sake of him and his sister. Apart from the drinking, his dad also was a womanizer. Ejike never wanted to be that kind of man. When he took his vows, it was for better or worse. The past six years for he and Amara had been great. Right now, the impending "worse" part scared him.

"Some men are just so cruel. There are people out there praying for children." His jaw tightened. "That should have brought you all closer together." Ejike walked over to favorite spot by the window and folded his arms across his chest. He was still shaking his head when he heard a whisper.

"I can't blame Afam. He tried, more than any man would." Chinelo lowered her eyes.

"No, he didn't. And you're too smart to make excuses for him," Ejike found himself taking her side. Nobody took his mother's side when his father had that temporary lapse in judgment that lasted eighteen months. Those were the months Ejike's dad decided to move in with another woman and practically forget his family. Ejike's jaw set when he remembered his painful past. Unlike Chinelo, his parents hadn't divorced, but that was mostly because his mother, for some reason, thought she needed his dad to survive.

"Obinna is not his son." Chinelo's voice was barely audible.

Ejike thought he didn't hear what she said. "Excuse me?"

"Obinna is not his son. He's yours."

CHAPTER 11

Amara shifted nervously in the tan colored chair. She could taste her heart in her mouth. Beads of sweat formed on her forehead, despite the coolness of the doctor's office. The pressure, the ridicule which had become too much to bear, would hopefully stop...today. Her mother-in-law was cordial, but always dropped snide comments here and there when the opportunity presented itself. Her husband's mother rarely visited them saying the house was too boring. Last year, when she did come, Amara remembered the tension in the kitchen as they baked for the church sale. Amara would have gladly done it herself, but the senior Mrs. Dike decided to help. That was a mistake.

"*Ehen* if only you had a child now, she would be helping you in the kitchen," her mother in-law had said.

Amara was certain that if her mother in-law had her way, Ejike would be a father by now. At this point, the woman could care less whether the child came from Amara or not.

Through it all, Ejike stood by her. But if she heard the line, "In God's time, honey" one more time, she would lose it. He was a man. He had no idea how it felt to look at him with the kids he coached and see the gleam of longing in his eyes. He would never admit that it bothered him that they still hadn't had a child.

One could say that her saving grace was that they lived in Dallas and not Lagos. Amara told herself so many times that if they lived in Nigeria, her in-laws would have packed her out of her husband's house by now or brought a woman they called fertile to have his kids.

Thank God for small graces. Guess the name, Amara, which meant God's grace, was really for me.

Her next thought was interrupted when the door opened. Dr. Trickman entered the room. His expression was blank. Amara's chest tightened. Another disappointment would be too much to bear. Now she wished she hadn't told Ejike not to come with her. His support would have been valuable right now. But then watching him try to hide his disappointment if the results were not favorable as she had done twice before would be too much. She clenched her fists to stop her hands from trembling. The doctor sat at his desk and his face cracked in a smile. Good smile, bad smile— Amara didn't know, but no need speculating.

"So doctor, tell me. The wait is killing me." Amara scooted forward in her chair. She fixed her eyes on the man before her. She didn't want to miss any expression that might cross his face.

"Amara, I have good news for you," the doctor said.

Amara was in a trance. She stopped listening at the word "good."

"Am I pregnant?" she asked, bouncing her knee up and down.

"Yes, you are. I'm pleased to tell you that the IVF was successful and you're five weeks pregnant." The doctor paused. "I'm sure Mr. Dike would be very happy with this news."

Tears rolled down Amara's face. She slid down from the chair to her knees. Raising her hands to the sky, she said, "Jehovah Almighty, God, I praise you. I give you all the glory. *I di ebube Baba.* You are a great God." She sat back down in her seat.

She couldn't wait to get home. This wasn't something that she was going to tell her husband over the phone. No, this had to be done over a candlelight dinner. That man had done what most men wouldn't do—stood by her through it all.

After a brief conversation on what to expect in the coming weeks and months, the doctor stood and walked around his desk. He stopped when he got to Amara. "Do you have any questions for me?"

Amara sighed. Even if she did, they eluded her now. There was tightness in her chest not from angst, but from joy.

"Uhmm... no. Can't think right now. The Lord has wiped the tears from my eye." She put her hand on her flat stomach and looked down. "You're sure everything is all right?" she asked. Amara still couldn't believe she was going to be a mother. A mother.

On the doctor's confirmation that she was fine, she walked out of his office to the nurse's station to schedule her next appointment.

Amara opened her car and got inside. She sat there and rested her head on the steering wheel and closed her eyes. After a few moments of silent prayer, she opened her eyes. The clock on the dashboard told her it was 3:00pm – 8:00pm in Nigeria. She took out her phone and dialed her mom.

The phone rang for about a minute with no answer. Amara almost gave up hope of getting an answer when her mother's voice came through the line. "Hello."

"Mummy, I was about to hang up. Are you in bed already?"

"No, I was talking to your dad in the study. How are you, my dear?

"Mummy, I'm sorry, I forgot my manners. Good evening, ma."

"*Ehen* my dear. You never call us this late. Is everything okay?" her mother asked.

"The devil has been put to shame. The God I serve has given me victory."

"What is it?" her mother asked.

Amara could feel her anxiety through the phone. "It worked mummy! It worked!" Amara screamed.

"The fertility procedure worked? I thought you didn't find out till next week."

"Yes oh...yes oh. It worked. I'm pregnant. Mummy, can you believe it?" Amara paused as her mother broke out into a song. Amara imagined her dancing around the center table of their Enugu living room.

"*The God that answereth by fire, He will be my God. The God that answereth by fire, He will be my God.*" Her mother sang. Amara joined her mother in praise.

After a couple of seconds, her mother asked, "Have you told your husband? What did your husband say? My enemies have been put to shame."

"No, I tried calling him once. But then I decided that this type of news I should give in person. I'm on my way home." She turned the key in the ignition and reversed the car. She was going to make a special dinner tonight.

"That man is so good to you. Not many men would have waited and stood by you this long. Especially an only son. God is good. Let me go tell your daddy," her mother said.

"Okay ma, I'll talk to you tomorrow. Remember, only tell daddy. I don't want anybody knowing 'til I'm well advanced."

"Okay, my darling. This is the time to intensify prayers. The devil is never idle so we should always be alert to his tricks."

"Yes ma, good night."

"'Nite, my dear," her mother said and they hung up the phone.

A FEW HOURS later Amara had showered and sparingly applied her favorite Victoria Secret mist behind her ears. The table was all set with pounded yam and *egusi* soup, and lit candles. She ran her finger through her hair to detangle her curls. She walked back to the kitchen when she heard the keys jiggle in the door. She secured the wrap on her silk lingerie and walked toward the door.

Ejike entered. Something about his aura was not right. Amara could see worry and concern written all over her husband's face. He locked the door, hugged her, and planted a kiss on her forehead.

"Welcome, honey. What's wrong?" she asked. "You look spent. Did you have a rough day?"

"Yes, I did."

Amara noticed the hesitation in his voice. She hoped nothing went wrong with the Neoh & Sons contract. But then again, he wasn't supposed to see them again for several weeks.

"You wanna talk about it?"

"No, babe. All I want to do is to go to sleep in your arms," Ejike said.

Amara smiled at the exact moment she saw that he became aware of what she was wearing. He smiled and pulled her close as they walked into the living room. He sat on the chair and pulled her into his lap.

"So, Mrs. Dike, what's going on? To what do I owe this beautiful sight?"

"Are you saying I'm not beautiful every night?"

"Far from it, but this is extra special." Ejike cupped her face and drew it towards his. His lips touched hers, gently at first, and then he began to invade her mouth. Amara wrapped her arms around her husbands' neck. He deepened the kiss.

She loved his gentleness, and then the pace changed. He was rougher than what she was used to. He slid his hands down her robe. Lips still locked, he hurriedly located her sash. This wasn't how she envisioned the evening. She broke free.

"Oh babe, come on..." Ejike protested.

"I have dinner all set. Freshen up while I re-heat it. I promise we can get back to dessert later." She winked.

Ejike let out a forced breath, set her aside and stood. His frustration was evident, but she would make it up to him.

THE KNOCK on the door alerted Ejike to his surroundings. The hot water had since turned cold as he stood underneath the jets lost in thought.

"I'll be right out," Ejike said loud enough for Amara to hear him above the music and running shower. He had put on the Winans, "It's Gonna Be Alright." He needed that confirmation right now, because he had no idea of how to deal with Chinelo's bombshell. It had rocked him to the core.

The reality of what he feared was even worse than he imagined. At first, he was in denial. After all, with Chinelo's record back then, he couldn't be the only one she slept with. Once she showed him the picture of the bright-eyed boy, there was no doubt Obinna was his. He had a son he knew nothing about, and really wanted a chance to get to know him. Chinelo must have seen his alerted stance at the realization that Obinna was indeed his. The look of satisfaction on her face was worrisome. She had kept this for years and would have never told him if Obinna didn't need medical treatment. Afam had walked out on her and Obinna after he had been tested for a bone marrow match, and it was discovered he couldn't have fathered the boy.

Now she wanted Ejike to be tested as a possible match and donor. There was no way he couldn't agree to help her son. *His* son. However, he couldn't consent to such a procedure without telling Amara. When Chinelo left his office, the air seemed to evaporate. He needed air and to clear his head. Not trusting himself to drive, Ejike decided to walk. He walked for miles. When his knees began to buckle, he turned back to get his car and drove home.

Ejike turned off the shower and stepped out of the stall. He dried his now pruned body, his head still spinning. How could this happen? It was just one night.

This would tear Amara apart. Not only did he sleep with her cousin, but that night had produced a seed. There was tangible evidence. The one thing they had been waiting on God for. He couldn't afford to lose her. He would sit her down and talk to her tonight. After dinner. Things were about to get ugly, but with God on his side, he hoped the Winans knew what they were saying —that it was going to be all right. He was not going to give up on his marriage without a fight.

Amara and Ejike were done eating and lingered over sparkling fruit juice.

"I'm mad at you. I've been waiting for you to ask me how the hospital visit went."

"That was today?" He feigned ignorance. He had totally forgotten because he was so wrapped up in his thoughts. Now everything was coming together. She had been giddier than usual and the dinner.

She hit him across the shoulder. "Are you kidding me right now?"

"I'm so sorry...so?" He tapped his feet absently.

Amara smiled. "Do you have names picked out?"

He remained calm. "Names?" Then it hit him. He jumped up and pulled her into his embrace. The tears running down her face confirmed his suspicion. He picked her up and twirled her around. She held on to him almost as hard as he held on to her.

He set her down, suddenly apprehensive that he might be hurting her.

"In about seven and a half months, you'll be a daddy."

"You mean we're pregnant?"

"Yes, we are honey. Yes, we are." Amara squealed as her husband picked her up again and twirled her around.

"I hope I didn't hurt you?" Ejike placed his hands on her stomach.

She laughed. "I'm pregnant honey, not sick." Then she paused. "The Lord has finally answered our prayers. Ejike and Amara Dike —first-time parents at last."

A tear escaped his lids. God sure did have a sense of humor. He had waited for this moment for so long. Now he had it, but under these circumstances. His confession had to wait as things were now complicated. He wished he could capture this moment in a bottle and take a whiff of it in the coming days. His breath caught as he imagined what the look of love in her eyes would turn to once she knew what he knew.

CHAPTER 12

It was barely noon and the sun was out in full effect. The scorching rays hit Ejike's head the second he stepped out of his car. He had just gotten the oil changed and tires rotated on the car for the Houston trip. This was the final stop—Target. He put his hands in his pocket to retrieve this list Amara had given him before she went to the salon that morning.

The Way Living Church couple's retreat was finally here. Ejike and other members of the Men's ministry had planned this three-day weekend to perfection. The ladies would be in for a treat and hopefully all of them would be fed by a word from Dr. Bradford.

It had been a toss-up if Dr. Bradford would make an appearance. He was quite a busy man and was currently on tour with his NY Times best-selling book. He and his wife had founded, 'Making It Work Ministries' twenty-five years ago.

Ejike had looked forward to this August event all year, but as each day turned to night he grew more afraid of what a new day would bring. It had been two weeks since Amara told him that he was going to father a child. What she didn't know was that unlike her, this wouldn't be his first time.

How he wished he had told Amara about Chinelo back then.

However, with a month to their impending nuptials and the fact that they had just gotten back together, that would have been disastrous. Now with this new development, and considering how hard it had been to get pregnant, Ejike couldn't bring himself to say anything. Perhaps he could wait until further along in the pregnancy. Maybe when Amara got out of the first trimester.

He walked towards the camping section to where the water bottle and food flasks were located. His phone buzzed.

Almost done with my hair, Amara texted.

Walking in the store now. Will be done soon. Ejike clicked the send button to reply. He shook his head, remembering Amara swearing off relaxers 'til the baby was born. She had started reading all kinds of books already. The excitement was infectious, although he really couldn't enjoy the moment because of the deception that loomed over his head. His conscience constantly nagged at him.

Ejike was the still puzzled about how one bad judgment call could leave him at a crossroads years later. He knew people that cheated all the time and never got caught. Ejike let out a labored breath as he turned into the aisle. But at the end of the day, the deed was done.

He had to do anything he could to help his son. Maybe he could get his bone marrow tested without Amara knowing. He quickly dismissed the notion. Hiding things was what got him into this mess in the first place. If he was found to be a match, there was no way he could have the procedure done without his wife knowing. He needed Amara's full support.

"*Help me, Lord,*" he prayed silently. He had never been so confused.

Ejike was also apprehensive about meeting a five-year old who had called someone else daddy all his life. He wanted to get to know him as his father, but Chinelo had insisted that Obinna didn't need to know just yet.

He picked up some snacks and made his way to the cashier. The retreat was at a resort in Houston, which was about a four hour journey from their Dallas home. If they left within the hour, they would make the 6:00pm check in time. There was a group dinner planned by seven thirty pm and as the chairman of the planning committee, he needed to be there on time.

Ejike made up his mind that he would try to enjoy the weekend. If he had a chance, he would talk to the pastor. He also intended to do a lot of prayer. He needed some serious intervention because when they got back, he'd have to set the record straight.

His phone rang. It was Nnamdi.

"*Oh boy how far naa?*" Nnamdi asked once Ejike answered the call. Despite their degrees, he and Nnamdi still loved to communicate in Pidgin English.

"*I dey* oh," Ejike unlocked the car door. "You know we're going on this couples' retreat today."

"How can I forget? It's all you've talked about. Send a prayer up to the Big Guy for me." Nnamdi's voice had a hint of sarcasm. He went to church, but didn't believe in doing anything extra. Ejike always told him it was because he didn't have a personal relationship with Christ yet. To which Nnmadi always replied, "I hear you."

"It's not that kind of party. We'll be praying, but mostly be bonding with our spouses, trying to rejuvenate our marriages," Ejike explained.

"Bonding, hmm. Make sure you get in as much as you can now because you'll need it when you tell Amara about Chinelo and your *pickin.*" Nnamdi laughed. "Wow. 'Your kid' has a nice ring to it, but I never expected it to be through Chinelo."

"I wonder why you think this is so funny. My marriage might be over and you're laughing."

"My bad. God does have a sense of humor *sha.*"

"Well, I'm not laughing. I'm in serious trouble here. I really want to step up and take care of my son, but Amara wouldn't be able to get past it."

"You're underestimating the love that lady has for you. And on top of that, she is saved," Nnamdi said.

"Saved doesn't mean she is a walk-over." Ejike shook his head. "She would never be able to forgive me. Not only don't I know the son I have, but Amara will make sure I don't see the unborn one either."

"Now you're just exaggerating. Amara would never do that." After a brief pause, Nnamdi continued. "But seriously bro, you need to tell her as soon as possible."

"I know that—"

"Especially if you need to get tested for the transplant."

Ejike heart constricted, causing him a sharp pain. "According to Chinelo, Obinna's doing quite okay now."

"With these things, you never know. It could turn into an emergency overnight. All I'm saying is… the earlier, the better," Nnamdi said.

Ejike turned his car into his subdivision. He hadn't thought of that. "I hear you, man. I plan to tell her when we get back. I just want to get this weekend over in peace." He stayed in the car and they chatted a little more before he hung up and headed inside.

Peace—how ironic. He knew for sure that the peaceful flow that reigned in his house was about to be overtaken by a severe thunderstorm.

AMARA WAS EXHAUSTED after the journey. She had resisted the urge to sleep in the car so Ejike wouldn't nod off as well. They were both tired from days of having to work hard to clear their schedules so they could have this day off. She planned on having an early night so she'd be refreshed for tomorrow's activities. As soon as Ejike slid their key to unlock the door on their fifth floor hotel room, Amara made a beeline for the bathroom.

A few minutes later she came out, refreshed, and moved across the room.

"This is nice." She pulled back the outer curtain. The city's skyline was littered with new architecture. The sun slowly bowed out to allow the moon to rise. Amara inhaled deeply. The room, which had an old fashioned feel, smelled of freshly cut roses. She walked over to the bed, sat, and slowly bounced on it. The sheets were made of high quality cotton. The walls were dark beige and all the furniture pieces looked like antiques. The walls were adorned with three, large, black-framed pictures of different scenes around the city of Houston.

"It better be. Don't you remember how much each couple had to pay for this trip?" Ejike kicked off his shoes and replaced them with slippers the hotel provided. He sat down on the chair by the bed and stretched out. Amara walked over to her husband and eased herself into his lap. She laid her head on his chest and just savored the moment. The scent of her husband's cologne was intoxicating. Life couldn't better and she owed everything to God. She rubbed her flat stomach and felt her husband's arms wrap around her.

"It's all for a good cause, honey. I'm glad we came. And considering our news, I'm going to have a marvelous time," Amara said.

I'm happy when you're happy," Ejike stroked her freshly woven hair.

Amara sat up and looked at her husband squarely. She cupped his face in her hands and planted a long, hard, kiss on his lips.

"Honey, I say this all the time and I pray to God you hear me. I'm so grateful that He gave me you. I thank you for not caving to the pressures back home. Encouraging me, when I couldn't encourage myself. I never had to worry about you and I'm so grateful," Amara said.

"We were made for each other. We vowed for better or worse and that how it's going to stay. I'm thankful He gave me you, too," her husband said. Amara could see raw desire in his eyes. He picked her up and placed her on the bed.

"Do we have time before the dinner?" she asked, giggling.

"We do, but even if we don't, they'll just have to start without us." Her husband began kissing and caressing her all over. She loved this man so much it hurt.

~

TWO HOURS LATER, with Ejike's hand on the small of Amara's back, they walked towards the elevators. She took a quick glance at her appearance through the doors. Since it was just a casual, get-to-know-you dinner, she had decided on deep blue, figure hugging, dress. Her baby bump was non-existent, so she might as well wear her clothes while she still could. On her feet, she wore black, low-heeled sandals.

The private dining room was simply elegant. Ejike turned to his wife and kissed her cheek.

"Okay babe, I'm going to leave you alone for some minutes. I have to make sure everything's been set up according to the instructions we gave."

"All right, honey. I'll mingle. I see Tonye."

Amara gawked at her husband as he walked away. His swag-o-meter was on a hundred. It got her every time. He had that aura of confidence about him that pulled her to him from the first day they met. The tapping of the microphone reeled her thoughts in. Amara looked up to see Pastor Harris flanked by Ejike and David Walker—Tonye's husband. They were standing in the middle of the room.

"Good evening, everyone. Glad you could make it," Pastor Harris said. "Welcome to our annual couples' retreat. The men have worked really hard this year to make this one for the record books."

There was applause around the room. Amara was excited. It

seemed that life was finally coming together. She and Ejike had no problems whatsoever. He loved her – she loved him. Life was great. To be able to get a weekend away to hear the word of God and fellowship with other couples was just the icing on the cake and she was looking forward to it. The best part of it was that they had secured relationship expert extraordinaire and man of God, Dr. Bradford. Amara still wasn't sure how they managed to do that. The story Ejike had told her was so simplistic that it almost didn't make sense. But that just showed that when God wants to work, He doesn't need anybody's help to do what needs to be done.

"Okay, ladies and gentlemen, with that we'll say a brief prayer and kick off the weekend. I want everyone to be expectant and receive the blessings that are about to be poured out into your life," Pastor Harris said. Everyone bowed their heads and he said a brief prayer.

"And the church said—"

"Amen," shouted the couples.

"Hey girl, you made it." Tonye said.

"Yes, I did." The ladies hugged each other. Amara looked around. Tonye was not with the new church member, Tia Jamesa.

"I thought you were coming with that new member, Tia?" Amara asked. Tonye was part of the outreach program, so was supposed to be in charge of making sure that new members knew what was going on.

"Hmm, girl, I don't think she's coming." Tonye looked around her as though she was about to release top secret information that nobody else was privy to.

"Why not? You said she had paid and everything."

"I know. I went over there, oh, my dear..." Tonye started.

Amara cackled. Although Tonye hadn't visited her native Nigeria in fifteen years, any time she wanted to tell what she had no business telling, she broke out in her native accent.

"There was no answer at their door. Then Pastor Paul told

David that there was a domestic violence call at the Jamesa house some days ago."

"Domestic violence. Edward hit Tia?"

"No! I heard Tia was wielding a knife because she found out about Edward's side chick," Tonye said.

Amara listened as Tonye rattled on, not stopping to take a breath. "You see, I guess because she just came from *Naija,* he thought she would be a walk-over. All these men go to Nigeria to marry because they want 'good' girls." Tonye made air quotation marks.

"Wow, that's unfortunate," Amara said.

"That's why I'm so thankful for my David. I can't do all this Naija man *wahala.*"

"Tonye, American men have issues, too. Men are men. We should pray for Tia and not talk about her."

"I agree. They are men, but you know the idea of marriage back home is sometimes warped. See now, David and I don't have kids yet, but we're happy. Let him have been from Nigeria. They would have expected I have a kid after nine months," Tonye said.

Amara saw the look of regret come over Tonye the minute the words fell out of her mouth. One Sunday last year, Tonye had found her crying in a stall in the women's bathroom. It was children's Sunday and the kids had just rendered the best song ever for their parents. It was too much for Amara to bear. That day, she had shared more than she intended to with Tonye about her mother-in-law and her struggle with infertility.

"I am so, so sorry. Me and my big mouth. I'm sorry. I'm sorry." Tonye pleaded.

Amara's smile was faint. "That's okay." She wasn't ready to disclose her present state, but in that moment she was so grateful that Tonye's comment wouldn't bring her tears. God had wiped them from her eyes.

"Have you tried to call Tia since then?" Amara asked.

"Yeah, but she isn't answering the phone. When we get back, I'll come get you so we can go over together."

As Tonye continued to make plans for them to see Tia, Amara spirit leaped in praise and thanksgiving. God had blessed her with the best man on earth. It was just by the grace of God and hard work that she and Ejike had stayed happy and completely committed to each other. Her joy was quickly replaced by sadness when she thought of Tia and Chinelo who had been unlucky in love. She sent a quick prayer to heaven for healing of their hearts. And for Him to send them their hearts desires.

CHAPTER 13

The following morning, David and Tonye smiled as Ejike and Amara hurriedly took a seat at the table they had reserved for them.

"I don't even want to know why y'all are late, but grab something to eat quickly. The workshop with Dr. Bradford is about to start."

"Good morning to you, too," Ejike said. He really wasn't about to paint the picture of him and his wife enjoying the privileges as man and wife that God allowed them.

"What are you having?" Amara asked Tonye.

"Grits, girl, and they are good. You should try some." Tonye put a spoonful of grits into her mouth.

Amara stood up and picked up the empty plates in front of Ejike and was about to head to the buffet table when he stopped her. "Don't worry. I got it. Just tell me what you want."

Amara rattled off her desired breakfast. Ejike smiled, noticing that her cravings were really beginning to kick in. She wanted things that didn't make any sense to him and he was sure it wouldn't to anyone else.

The couples ate breakfast over light banter. That seemed to be the atmosphere in the room. When they were done, Amara excused herself to the ladies' room for what Ejike thought was the umpteenth time that morning. He watched her walk away and sent up a prayer of thanks for the last eight years—two spent courting and six as man and wife—with her and asked for grace for the days and years to come.

When the gospel trio stepped on the stage, Ejike looked around the room to see if Amara was on her way back. He began to bob his head to the music as the chords of the Hillsong classic, "Majesty" came on. He prayed along to the words of the song, *"Your grace has found me just as I am, empty handed but alive in your hands..."*

Ejike was still deep in prayer mode when he felt a hand rubbing his back. Amara had slipped into the seat beside him. He looked at her and a tear escaped him. She raised her finger and wiped it from his cheek. She smiled at him. He kissed her on her forehead. Their gaze into each other's eyes was interrupted by applause as the singers finished the song.

Soon after, David left the table to go and introduce Dr. Bradford.

As the man of God stepped on the stage, everyone stood to their feet and applauded. After a few moments, he asked everyone to be seated.

"Let's bow our heads in prayer and commit today to the Lord," Dr. Bradford said. "Almighty, Omnipotent God, we acknowledge your presence in this place. Please open our hearts and our minds that we might hear a word from you, in Jesus' name."

"Amen," the crowd answered.

"Okay, ladies and gentlemen, praise the Lord! Hope you all are having a nice time. I'm honored to be here today. Any time I'm offered the opportunity to use my ministry to teach, I'm grateful to God." Dr. Bradford took a swig of water from his water bottle.

"Today we are going to talk about marriage and love. But wait, before you even think it, this is not about the popular Paul passage, 'love is kind, love is ...'you know. Although all that is true, I want to talk about marriage and making it work. So let's start from the basic misconceptions. The first one we will address is the popular saying, "my spouse completes me" or the one that makes me cringe, "marriage is fifty/fifty." Sometimes when we say things, we don't understand the real meaning. Each one of us was created in the image and likeness of God. God is complete all in Himself and He has made us that way so nobody completes you. You complement each other."

There was applause and shouts of, "That's good," from the crowd.

"That brings me to that second saying. Since we are all complete beings when we come into a marriage we have to come as one hundred percent. Bring one hundred percent each to the table to make a perfect whole.

"When you come together, everyone has to be willing to put something into the empty basket called marriage. When I first met my wife, she introduced me to this concept, but I didn't believe her. She had to teach me that marriage was an empty bowl, and each of its occupants bring the love, peace, harmony. Anything you want to take out of the marriage, you have to be willing to do the work to put it in there. And how do you put in there?"

There was murmuring in the room.

The man of God drank some more water. "Through love that is...not that lusty stuff. Because that will pass and the true love will remain. True love is that love that made Jesus Christ leave all glory and come down to die for our sake. You see, true love is a doing love. It's not a feeling. It's not goose bumps. It's not heart palpitations. True love is doing. What are you doing to make sure your marriage bowl stays filled with all those things you long and desire for? It's hard work, but the key is, two people totally committed to God. I love this quote from James C. Dobson, "Don't marry the person you think you can live with. Marry only the individual you think you can't live without.

"Once you do that, keep God in the center. You can weather any storm. And that is what "Making It Work" is all about."

Ejike knew that he had married the one he couldn't live without. He prayed that when he showed Amara his hidden hand that he was the one she couldn't live without either.

Dr. Bradford taught them some more principles of a lasting marriage. He even used the popular 80/20 rule for illustration. After two hours of teaching and couple exercises, he wrapped up with a prayer.

The crowd stood and cheered as Dr. Bradford left the stage.

CHAPTER 14

The rise of the sun brought fresh new possibilities. Amara rose from the bed with a satisfied glow on her face. She stretched her arms up in the air, feeling grateful for this well-deserved rest and the awesome talk yesterday by Dr. Bradford. It fed her soul. She and Ejike had a romantic dinner afterwards. She smiled when she remembered how he expressed his love to her again in such a childlike manner. It almost scared her. If she didn't know him so well, she'd think that something was amiss.

She stretched her body again and looked at the dent her husband's absent head had left on the pillow. He did tell her yesterday that he and a couple of the other men would be going to jog in the morning and have a final meeting before everyone left later in the day. She picked up the note he placed on the pillow. She beamed in anticipation of reading sweet little nothings from her husband.

Good morning, babe. Hope you slept well. Went down to exercise and hang out with the guys before breakfast, see you soon! ~ Ejike

Amara forced herself to get up after a brief conversation with God, thanking Him for this day and this weekend.

She and Tonye had decided to go and pay Tia a visit the next evening. She had finally answered her phone and said everything was all right, but they wanted to see for themselves.

Amara laid out what she and Ejike would wear and decided to start packing for the return trip. She stopped when her phone rang. It was Chinelo.

"Sis, what's going on?" Amara asked.

"Ah nothing oh. I was just checking up on you guys. Are you on your way home?" Chinelo asked.

Amara detected unease in her cousin's voice. "*O di kwa nma?* Is everything okay?"

"Yes, don't mind me. What about Ejike?" Chinelo asked hurriedly.

Amara laughed. "Since when did you and Ejike become *paddy paddy*? Ever since the concert, you've been asking of him like he's your best friend."

Chinelo hesitated. "Is he not my in-law? I can ask about him now, *haba*."

"Anyway, I'm glad both of you are friends again." Amara folded the last piece of clothing in the suitcase and filled Chinelo in on Ejike's whereabouts. The cousins talked a little bit more, made plans for the upcoming weekend, and then hung up.

Amara felt something wasn't right, but Chinelo wasn't telling her what. Maybe it was Obinna. When she got back to Dallas, she would make sure Ejike accompanied her to see the boy.

An hour later, dressed in a plum, three-quarter sleeve blouse and a pair of jeans, Amara peered closer to the mirror to make sure her eyeliner hadn't smeared. It hadn't. She was twisting the top off the lip gloss when the door opened. She smiled and turned around.

"There goes my man. I thought you forgot about me."

"Never," Ejike said with a smile as he walked towards her and gave her a kiss on the cheek. "How is my baby today?"

"I'm good. I couldn't wait any longer, so I ordered room service. Now that the two of us are fed, all is right with the world."

Amara laughed. She winked at her husband, rubbing her stomach in a circular manner.

"Great, I'm glad. I'm not really hungry any way. Let me take a shower and we can hit a few of Houston's hot spots before we start the journey home.

"Sounds good."

~

IT WAS EIGHT O' clock before they walked into their four bedroom home. *At home at last.* Amara walked out of the bathroom after what seemed like the longest shower ever.

"I trust there won't be a drop of hot water left for me," Ejike teased.

"There is, but even if there isn't, in Ihiala, didn't you bathe with cold water every morning?" Amara laughed and Ejike joined in with the reference to his childhood in his village.

"You're dissing Ihiala *o kwa ya*? Right? Don't forget Ihiala was never this cold."

"What are you talking about? Isn't this summer? My friend, go and shower so we can eat." Amara waved a hand, dismissing his concern.

Ejike was on his way to the bathroom when he stopped. He pulled out his phone from his pocket. He tried to power it on, but failed.

"Babe, please charge my phone for me while I shower. It died when I was out with the fellas and since you were with me, I didn't bother charging it."

"Okay, leave it on the bed. Hurry up in the shower. I want to be relaxed on the couch before the new movie on UP starts," she said. UP TV was her new addiction. It was a new inspirational station that showed only uplifting movies and shows.

Ejike tossed it on the bed and headed towards the bathroom. Amara crossed over to the other side of the bed to pick up his phone. A few minutes after she plugged in the charger, the phone buzzed. Amara ignored it and proceeded to get her clothes ready for work the next day. *He'll get it when he comes out.*

Amara walked to the dresser for her head wrap. It was an unspoken rule that neither of them answered the other's phone. Not that they couldn't—they just never did. There was a second buzz, then shortly after, a third. Amara was about to ignore it again, when the phone started to ring. Whoever it was, the person was desperately trying to get in touch with Ejike. Her curiosity was piqued.

Amara walked across the room to answer the call, but by the time she got to the phone, it had stopped ringing. Immediately, the phone started ringing again. Amara pressed the talk button to say something when she recognized the voice on the other end of the line was in a frenzy.

"I've been trying to reach you. Why are you not returning my calls?" the caller asked.

Amara recognized the voice immediately as Chinelo's. A thousand questions came flooding into her head. Chief among them was, why was Chinelo calling her husband? And why was Ejike avoiding her calls? Just as Amara was about to open her mouth, Chinelo continued.

"I know that you're there with your wife and all, but I really need you or I wouldn't be calling."

Amara opened her mouth to speak, but nothing came out.

Chinelo blurted out, "Your son is in the hospital."

Apparently frazzled by the lack of response, Chinelo shouted. "Look Ejike, I really didn't want you to meet your son like this, but we need you here, especially now that you know about Obinna. Find something to tell Amara. In case you forgot, he is the only child God has given you."

Amara felt her breakfast and all the junk food she had eaten along the way, come up to her throat. She was about to throw up. She looked at the caller ID to make sure she wasn't dreaming. It was Chinelo. She checked the phone again, to make sure it was Ejike's. The phone slipped from her grasp and landed on the floor with a thud. Uncontrollable tears started to rush down her cheeks. Her heart pounded in her chest. Suddenly it seemed like the room was closing in on her.

The bathroom door opened and Ejike entered the room. Amara turned to look at him, her lips trembling, her body shaking all over. He closed the gap between them.

"Babe, what's wrong?" he asked.

She stepped back. He had a puzzled look on his face. "Babe, what is it?" he asked again when he saw the phone on the floor. He picked it up and she stepped back. Amara saw him quickly go through the phone. She saw the blood drain from his face. That was the confirmation she feared.

A voice that she didn't recognize as her own finally said, "You have a son? With Chinelo?"

CHAPTER 15

With one blink of an eye, Amara opened the door and was gone. What had just happened? Ejike picked up his phone and saw that he had three unread text messages. He opened them one after the other. They were all from Chinelo telling him that she had to take Obinna to the emergency room the night before. Apparently, he had started to feel faint and dizzy with chest pain. Because of his low blood levels the doctors had decided to keep him for observation overnight. He was dehydrated, but didn't need blood at this time.

Ejike could feel his brain being knocked around in realization of what had just happened. His worst nightmare was now a reality. Life as he knew it was about to change. He had to catch up with Amara. A range of emotions overtook him as he frantically reinforced his towel. He needed to get to her, and fast.

He felt his gut tighten as he opened the door. She was standing near the top of the stairs, rubbing her stomach. It was as though she was trying to draw strength from their unborn child. The tears that flowed down her cheeks caused him to flinch. She must have sensed his presence as she looked up and stared at him, about to make her way down. Fear gripped him and he felt like he had aged a thousand years in the few minutes that Amara had bolted from the room.

"Baby, please let me explain." Ejike closed the gap between them. His comment was met with silence. That worried him. He expected her to be outraged, but she was too calm for his liking. "Amara please look at me, I can explain."

"Ejike, there is nothing to explain. Unless you're trying to tell me that what I heard was all a big joke," she said. "If you can't tell me that, then there's nothing to explain."

"Amara, it's not at all like you think it is." He stretched out his hand to touch her.

She moved back, teetering on the edge. "Don't touch me." Her warning was low, but he felt the venom. "You and Chinelo? How? When? Where? I can't even get the thought to form in my head properly."

"Amara hold on. It was a long time ago. You and I had a brief break up. I swear I knew nothing about the child until recently."

"Brief break up? When?" she asked. "You mean that time when I found out I might not be able to have kids? Those four weeks? Really?"

The feeling of shame washed over him. Even to his ears, it sounded terrible. It was a moment of weakness and he needed desperately for her to hear him out. "Yes," he said under his breath.

"Wow, and you didn't tell me?" she asked, her voice cold as ice. "Here I was, silly me, trying to bring you two back together. Trying to restore your friendship and you're secretly laughing behind my back."

"That's not how it is at all. Please calm down."

"Calm down? Calm down? I need to get out of here." Amara looked around wide eyed.

"Amara, wait..." Ejike grabbed her arm.

Amara whipped around suddenly. "I told you not to touch me." She ran down the stairs.

Ejike rushed down after her, "Amara, Amara, *biko nu*. Please, Amara wait."

Amara looked back at him as she struggled to put on her jacket. The look of love she wore a few minutes earlier was replaced by something else. Disdain. Contempt. Hurt.

He opened his mouth to speak, but before he could completely form his thoughts, the front door slammed. She was gone.

~

AMARA WAS LOST. She looked around and tried to get her bearings. The environment was unfamiliar. She had no idea how long she had been walking. She felt bare, insecure. The two people she had trusted the most had sent her world crashing down. She touched her stomach. What should be a time of joy for her had turned to agony. Her unborn child wouldn't be Ejike's firstborn. He already had one.

How could I have been so stupid? Ejike and Chinelo's budding friendship suddenly changed and neither of them wanted to talk about it. A classic sign of shadiness.

Tears blurred her vision as she continued to walk aimlessly. She spotted a gas station across the street where she could ask for directions. Her knees were weak and her stomach felt sore. She needed to lie down, get under the covers, and never come out.

How could he do this to her? How could Chinelo do this to her? She felt numb. She stood at the pedestrian stop, waiting for the perfect time to cross the road. Her mind travelled back to the phone call. *Find something to tell Amara. In case you forgot, he is the only child God has given you.* She was the stepmother of her nephew. She felt nauseous.

"God, how could You allow this to happen to me? How? Were You asleep?" Amara shouted, not minding the audience. She thought she saw the light change. She stepped into the road and was startled by the blaring horn of an eighteen wheeler. She stepped back just in time. Amara felt the weight of the world on her shoulders. She sat down on the pavement. Tired. Humiliated. She allowed the tears to flow. Her life was over. Nothing made sense anymore.

EJIKE'S GUT clenched and sweat rolled down his temples like water had been poured on him. He paced the living room again. It had been an hour since Amara left and he had no idea where she was. In her haste to leave, she had left her phone and her car keys. He had gone upstairs to put on some clothes and combed the subdivision, but couldn't find her.

He got down on his knees and rested his elbows on the couch. "Lord, please help me. I'd never forgive myself if anything happened to her or the baby she's carrying." He looked up at the wall clock again—9.30pm. He heard a car pull up in the driveway. He recognized the car as being one of their neighbor's. It was Amara. He mouthed a, "thank You" to heaven and ran out of the house.

Amara's hair was disheveled and her skin was pale. It looked like the blood had been drained out of her. She walked toward the house bent over. Ejike's brows came together in a frown. His heart bled at the pain he had caused her. He moved closer to help her.

"Don't touch me," she said in a voice he didn't recognize.

His strides were guarded as he followed her closely. They entered the house in silence.

"Amara..."

She put on foot on the stairs and clutched the rail. She turned to look at him. The daggers in her eyes told him everything that was in her heart. "Ejike, leave me alone. Please."

Amara began climbing the stairs and then yelled out in pain. Ejike rushed to her side. In one swift motion, he carried her to the couch. He placed a pillow under her head. She coiled in a fetal position, whimpering and clutching her stomach. It took a minute for his mind to figure out what to do. He pulled her into his lap and noticed a dark circle forming at the spot she had occupied. Her whimpers changed to labored moans. Ejike whipped out his phone and called 911 immediately. He held the phone with one hand and cradled her with the other. Tears dropped from his eyes. *God, please, this can't be happening. This can't be happening.*

THE HOSPITAL WAS SUPPOSED to be a place of healing, but right now it smelled like death. Ejike paced the waiting area. He recalled the fifteen minute ambulance ride from the house to the hospital—the longest minutes of his life. During the short ride, he was unaware of how many times he had called on Jesus to help him. His heart pounded in his chest as Amara was wheeled to the ER. It had been thirty minutes and nobody had come out to talk to him.

He walked up to the reception area when a nurse came through the double doors.

"You came with Amara Dike, right?"

"Yes," he replied.

"Follow me." She turned and went through the double doors.

On the way to the room, the nurse told him Amara had been given some painkillers and was resting. Ejike heart crumpled when he saw Amara. She looked fragile and avoided eye contact with him. She hadn't looked him in the eyes since the horrible incident. He tried to hold her hand, but she flinched and turned on her other side.

Ejike didn't even know how he would begin to explain, but

what he did know was that he would fight for his marriage with ever fiber in his being.

God, please give me the wisdom to give my wife exactly what she needs right now. Protect my unborn child. He was just about to say, "Amen," when the door opened.

The doctor walked in. The look on his face was not good. Amara turned around to face him. Ejike walked closer.

"Hi, I'm Doctor Vorster." He extended his hand and Ejike took it. The doctor looked at Amara. "I see our patient is resting."

"Yes, she is" Ejike said.

Amara wore a blank expression.

"So doctor, is everything alright?" Ejike asked anxiously.

The doctor looked at Amara, then at him. The light in his face suddenly dimmed. "I'm afraid I have bad news." Ejike heard Amara gasp. He walked over to hold her hand. She didn't resist.

"Please, what is it? Is the baby okay?" Amara asked faintly. The tone of her voice pierced Ejike heart. It was laced with pain.

"I'm sorry, but you lost the baby," he said.

Ejike felt Amara's hand slip away from his. Tears began to roll down her cheeks. She let out a scream.

"I'm so sorry. We will keep you for observation overnight and give you something to ease the pain," the doctor said. He nodded to the nurse and they both left the room.

The silence when they left was deafening. The only thing that could be heard was Amara's whimpering. Ejike studied her for a minute, not sure what to do. He walked over to the side of the bed where she turned her face.

"Amara," he said softly. *God, You need to help me now, please. I need wisdom.*

"Amara, *biko nu,* don't cry, please. I'm here. Please, I'm sorry. I love you very much. I'm so sorry."

He sat on the bed. She placed her head on his lap and he stroked her hair. Amara didn't say a word. The only sound Ejike could hear from her were gut wrenching sobs. Her hot tears began to seep through his pants.

What have I done? Not only had he betrayed his wife, but his infidelity was now the cause of them losing their child. Despite the warmth of her head on his lap right now, he knew that the days ahead would be colder than the white walls in this hospital room.

Amara leaned back into the pillows. During the course of the night, the nurse had come in a number of times to check on her. Each time, she announced that Amara's vitals were perfect. That was more than Amara could say for her heart. Her peaceful life was now playing out like a horror movie, and she was stuck with no exit. Thinking about it had her stomach in a knot. And to top it off, the only thing she could hold on to—her baby—had been taken away from her. She was grateful for Ejike's absence this morning. Because if she heard him call her "babe" like there was nothing wrong one more time, she couldn't be held responsible for what she might do. Right now, she could do without breathing the same air as him.

Amara exhaled. She needed to wash her face. She got up from the bed and walked over to the sink. In autopilot, she brushed her teeth and washed her face. The cold water refreshed her. She stared at her reflection in the mirror.

"Father, what did I ever do to deserve this? Why would You allow this cup to come my way? I have served you faithfully since my teens. Why *ehen*?"

Amara was angry. *How can you stand by and allow Chinelo to sink her claws into my husband? To top it off, You gave her a child. Meanwhile You have left me barren. What's the point of holding on to You if You would me leave out there to wolves in sheep's clothing?"* She lifted her eyes lifted towards the ceiling.

The crampy pain in her stomach forced her back to the bed. She sat there and stared out the window. Her mood was as overcast as the grey skies outside. She blinked back a tear. They had been flowing steady the whole night. At this rate, she might dry up her supply. Even though her unborn baby was barely eight weeks, they had formed a bond. She knew what she would have liked the child to be called, although it was customary that the child's name come from Ejike's dad. Before she had time to marinate in her blessing, she was mourning a loss. As a matter of fact, several losses—her unborn child, her marriage, and her perfect life.

Her room door opened. Ejike entered the room with two cups of coffee. His presence irritated her. She knew the disgust in her eyes was apparent.

"Babe, good morning. How are you feeling?" He placed the cups on the end table.

She remained silent. Amara couldn't believe he was going to act like they didn't have a mountain between them.

"Ejike, you don't deserve to know how I'm doing. In fact, I don't want to talk to you. Go away." Fresh tears rolled down her face.

"Babe," Ejike said. "Please don't cry." He walked over to comfort her, but she pushed him away.

"Don't." Her body was visibly shaking.

"I'm sorry."

"You're sorry? That's it? You're sorry. I can't believe this is happening to me." She wished she would wake up and this would all be a bad dream. But she had pinched herself earlier, and this was very much her reality.

"Babe, please let's get you out of here and we'll talk on the way home."

"There is nothing to talk about. Go be with Chinelo and her son."

"Amara, you don't mean that. I didn't know about a son. I swear to you." He raised his right hand in the air.

"So when exactly did you find out that *you* had a son?" she asked with her hands folded across her chest. She didn't miss his obvious attempt to downplay the fact that the child was his as well.

Where is this doctor so I can go home, abeg? She needed the comfort of her own bed. The bed that Ejike wouldn't be sleeping in any time soon.

He remained silent.

"Oh, you can't talk?

"Amara, calm down. You're not that strong. I'll answer all your questions. Let's get out of here first," he whispered.

There was a sharp knock on the door and the doctor entered.

"Good morning. How are you feeling this morning?" Dr. Vorster asked.

Amara gave a favorable reply.

He spent the next couple of minutes looking at her chart. "Everything seems okay. I'm going to write you a prescription for pain and discharge you."

Turning to Ejike, the doctor continued, "This is a very trying time emotionally and physically. Make sure she has enough rest, at least for the next couple of days." Then the doctor smiled. "And a lot of love and care."

Amara almost choked on her muffled laughter. *Love. Hmm...yeah right.*

THERE WAS complete silence during the drive home, with both of them lost in thought. Ejike understood her need for space and would give it to her, but he needed her to give him a chance to explain. Something snapped in her and after the doctor left, she decided she no longer wanted to hear what he had to say. He knew he wasn't in a position to demand anything, so all he could do was hope and pray. It was a miracle that she let him drive her home. He kept the radio on the gospel station. Hopefully something she heard would speak to her. He knew it was manipulative, but he needed all the help he could get.

When Amara was asleep earlier in the hospital, he was able to call Chinelo. She was about to go off on a tangent, but he quickly told her this was not the time and asked about his son. Obinna was doing better and had been discharged earlier.

Ejike regretted the path he had chosen. Covering up and hiding his mistake, and shielding Amara from the truth was the reason his life was a royal mess right now. Ejike didn't know whether he and Amara could get back to the place they once were. One thing was for sure, he wasn't letting either his wife or his son go. There was only one person that didn't fit into this equation and that was Chinelo.

After dropping Amara off at the house, Ejike went to the pharmacy to fill her prescriptions. On the way back from the pharmacy, Ejike called Nnamdi. "O boy, this Chinelo stuff just got real."

"What happened? How was the retreat?" Nnamdi asked.

Ejike spent the next few minutes bringing him up to speed on the events of the weekend.

"Oh my God. Amara miscarried?" Nnamdi asked.

'Yes, "Ejike said. He wound down the window and stayed in the car to talk to Nnamdi.

"Oh man...this is some serious *yawa* oh. How is Amara?"

"Physically, she'll be okay. Emotionally, I have no idea," Ejike said.

"What do you mean, you have no idea? Haven't you guys talked? Didn't you tell her how and when everything happened?" Nnamdi fired the questions at him. "Not that that will excuse your deception, but the fact you didn't know about the boy and the thing with Chinelo was when she had called off the wedding should account for something."

"At this point, nothing I could say would ease the pain." Ejike sighed.

"That's not good. Amara loves you very much, but you've got your work cut out for you. First you need to straighten Chinelo out. Then pray to your God, because you are going to need Him," Nnamdi said.

There was an awkward silence between the two men. Ejike said goodbye and they hung up the phone. Bracing himself, he pressed the garage door opener. The next time he saw Chinelo, it would be to let her know she was no longer running things.

He was.

Chapter 17

The couple of weeks that followed did not go at all how Ejike had envisioned. Amara didn't eat much, and she barely came out of her room. When she did come out, she walked around lifeless. Her fire, her spunk seemed to dissipate. All she offered him in speech was "Uhum," "Ehen," "Yes," or "No." He would feel so much better if she would scream, shout, or break something. That he could deal with. But this silence was killing him. It was deafening and he was alarmed.

She wouldn't do anything silly, now would she? She is a woman of God after all.

Life was at a standstill because she refused to talk. He ached because he saw her aching, but she refused to let him make an attempt to ease the pain.

He had been flexing his days at work, but today he had a big strategy meeting with his boss for the upcoming Michigan trip with Neoh & Sons.

He rose from the queen-sized bed in the guest room. On his own, he decided to relocate from the master suite. Not that he thought for a second that Amara would let him sleep next to her. He put on his shirt and made his way down stairs. He had to remember that his strength came from God. And He was able to do anything, fix any situation. He loved his wife, and he wanted to get to know his son. But there was no way he could do it on his own.

Ejike entered into his study and sat behind the desk. He contemplated for a minute then picked up the Bible. He didn't know where to start or what to look for, but he needed something. In addition to the predicament in his home, today he planned on seeing Chinelo and his son. They had arranged to meet mid-morning. Chinelo had kept the boy hidden like a pawn.

If his life was such a mess, he had to at least get to know Obinna. He needed God to go before him. Flipping through the pages of the marked up Bible, he landed on Psalm 50 verse 15 *"and call on me in the day of trouble; I will deliver you, and you will honor me."* Ejike read the chapter, then the verse, over and over again. He bowed his head and prayed. "Father God, please come to my aid. I know I'm the sole cause of my problem. I should have listened all these years, but I didn't. I'm sorry, but I need You. Give me strength, Father. Give me wisdom. Fix this thing Father, please. In Jesus' name. Amen."

Ejike browsed his iPod for just the right song and found, "He is Good" by VaShawn Mitchell. It was 6:00 am and he didn't want to wake Amara, so he put in his earplugs and listened to the words of the song. He listened to it with a deeper appreciation for the lyrics. He played the song a couple more times before he got up. With renewed energy, he turned off the light and went into the kitchen to make some tea. Amara loved drinking French Vanilla Lipton tea first thing in the morning.

Some minutes later, he knocked on the bedroom door. He got no response and opened it. Amara had the covers over her head. He set the steaming cup down and walked over and turned the television off. She must have dozed off and left it on. He walked over to her side of the bed. He sat down on the edge and stroked her hair.

She shifted. She opened her eyes and he could tell all the painful memories flooded back because her body stiffened. She sat up in the bed, drawing the comforter up to her chin.

"Good morning," she said.

"Good morning, babe. Did you sleep well?"

"Uhum."

There goes that word again.

Ejike stood and handed her the tea.

"Thank you."

She cupped the mug with both hands and sipped it slowly. There was an awkward silence in the room.

"Amara, I need to go into the office today for a strategy meeting."

She didn't say anything.

"I wouldn't go if I could miss it. But you know this Neoh & Sons thing is huge." He waited for a response. When he didn't get any, he stood up.

"Do you need anything?"

"No."

"Ok, I'll let you rest. If you need anything, please call me."

Ejike could feel the gulf between them expanding and he had no idea how to mend it. But one thing was sure, he could no longer live like this. He kissed her on the forehead, professed his love again, and walked out.

Some hours later, Ejike followed the directions of the GPS and brought his Range Rover to a halt in front of Chuck E Cheese. Chinelo had suggested they meet there so that they would have a chance to talk while Obinna played. He got out of the car and made his way into the building. It didn't take long for him to find Chinelo.

"Hello," she said as he approached. He could tell from her voice that she was nervous. That was good.

"Hello, how are you?"

"We are okay, oh. Just as you left us," she said, drawing out the "oh" for dramatic effect.

"Chinelo, cut it out..."

"How is Amara?"

"How do you think?"

"Sarcasm doesn't suit you. Anyway, it's high time she knew. I mean she's my blood, but my son comes first and he needed you."

Ejike looked at her, bewildered. He wondered if she knew about the miscarriage whether she'd be this insensitive. Somehow, he knew it wouldn't make a difference.

"A son you haven't let me see? By the way where is he? I told you to bring him." Ejike looked around.

"He's over there playing." She smiled slyly.

Ejike had no idea what her smile was about, but he was about to squash it. "Chinelo, let's get one thing straight. There is space for only one woman in my life and that is Amara. Always has been."

Chinelo opened her mouth to speak, but he raised his hand to silence her. "Let me finish. I made a mistake sleeping with you. Then I kept it a secret. My worst mistake was not telling her about Obinna the minute I found out. But that's not a license for you to slip in. I want a relationship with my son and that's it."

"You can't just come and demand stuff." Chinelo's tone told him she hadn't expected his reaction.

"Look, I'm tired of playing with you. You keep Obinna a secret all these years, and then suddenly show up with him. I owe you nothing. If it's me you want, you're barking up the wrong tree." Ejike paused. "As for the transplant, I'll talk to Amara and get tested." He didn't know how much more of this he could take, but she was beginning to get on his nerves. He had no one to blame but himself, but that stopped today.

"So, since he exists I want to see him. Now!"

"Okay." Chinelo got up and walked slowly to the play area.

Ejike pulled out his phone and checked it again. He had called

Amara earlier, but the call went straight to her voice mail. He followed it with a text, neither of which she had responded to.

That morning, he told himself that he could no longer live like this and he meant it. When he got home tonight, they would sort this thing out. Ejike was still deep in his thoughts when Chinelo approached with a boy who was his spitting image. The resemblance gave Ejike goose bumps. He was nervous and he could tell the boy was, too.

Ejike stooped down in front of the boy so they could be on eye level. "Hi. How are you?"

Obinna turned to his mother who nodded, giving him permission to answer. "Fine."

Father and son remained silent. Neither seemed to know what to say next.

Chinelo spoke, "Obi, remember I told you that some of mummy's friends lived here?"

Obinna nodded.

"Well, this is one of them. Say hi to Uncle Ejike," Chinelo said.

Ejike didn't want to be known as Uncle anything. But he understood the need to slowly introduce Obinna to another person as his father. After all, he grew up knowing Afam as his father.

On Ejike's prompting, Chinelo walked over to the counter. He wanted time to be alone with Obinna. For the next half hour, Ejike tried to get the boy to talk, but he was shy and reserved. Not like any five year-old he knew, but this was just their first encounter. He planned on remedying that.

Some time later, Ejike turned to Chinelo when Obinna was out of earshot. "We need to talk about arrangements."

"What arrangements?" she asked with a raised eyebrow.

"Excuse me? Didn't you hear what I said about getting to know Obinna? What did you really hope to accomplish coming here with him? "

"I don't know. I'm just tired of being handed the crumbs all the time. I want what's mine."

"And what is yours? Me? I've asked you this before – are you insane?" Ejike raised his index finger to his temple.

Chinelo was silent.

Ejike continued, "I'm going to talk to Amara. I want Obinna to spend a weekend with us, sometime soon."

"Alone? Ha, no. I don't know what that woman will do to my son."

"Chinelo, Amara isn't like that and you know it. She's hurt right now, but that's my business. Second, if he's going to be around me, he's going to be around my wife. So, again I ask—if that's not what you want, why did you come?" Ejike shoved his hands in his pocket. He could feel his blood rising.

Before Chinelo could respond, Obinna came running over to where they were talking. "Mummy, can we go now?"

"Okay, baby, we're going to leave."

Ejike looked around the parking lot, "Did you drive? You want me to drop you off?"

"I called a taxi. Obinna has half-day camp he goes to with his cousins to keep him busy. It's not far from here. I'll drop him off, then go home."

"Okay, I'll give you a call soon to make arrangements," Ejike said. He saw the unease on her face.

"What?" he asked

"Amara. I don't know how to face her. I had it all figured out in my head, but now..."

"Don't look at me. I'm not her favorite person now, either." He paused. "But I know you didn't expect her to be all smiles. Since this is your show, you should have a game plan, right?"

Chinelo remained silent.

Ejike couldn't be bothered with her conscience right now. He had his own problems to worry about.

~

Amara slumped on the light toned sofa with her legs folded under her. The plush couch contrasted with the rich, dark, hardwood floors. She flipped through the channels aimlessly. Right after Ejike left, she put on her robe and went downstairs. Her growling tummy had alerted her that she needed food. For the past two weeks, her appetite was non-existent. She nibbled on her last piece of toast and settled on the Lifetime channel. She looked over at her mini home office in the corner. She hadn't been to her real office in a while. She missed it, but knew she couldn't be productive if her life was in shambles.

Ejike had tried to talk to her, but she really didn't want to hear what he had to say. It wouldn't change anything anyway, so how ever it happened was irrelevant. Life really didn't have any meaning for her anymore.

The phone rang. Amara threw the blanket to the side and went to answer it.

The caller ID showed a toll free number she didn't recognize. "Hello," Amara said.

"Hello, may I speak to Amara Dike," the caller said.

"Speaking."

"Hi, ma'am, this is Rosalina from Travel Made Easy. How are you doing today?"

"Who?" *I really don't have time for telemarketers today.*

"Ma'am, we spoke about three months ago and you were interested in a vacation package. It was for the Serenity Resort in Spain."

Amara remembered. She and Ejike had agreed that once the Neoh & Sons project was over, they'd go away on a romantic vacation.

"I'm calling to follow up. Did you need any additional information?"

"No, thank you. I'm no longer interested." Amara hung up the phone before the lady responded.

Amara snapped out of the shock she had been floating in since her world had been turned upside down. Her denial dissipated as her insides began to rumble with rage. She paced back and forth. Her life had been perfect. She didn't have a child, but she had love. She had hope. She had joy. The numbness she felt turned into a blinding anger for the two people that had caused her grief. She was not going to lie down and take it anymore.

It was time she paid the serpent who had entered her garden of love a visit. It was time to see Chinelo.

AMARA TOOK A LONG HOT SHOWER. As the jets sprayed her body, she felt like all the self-pity was being washed away. What couldn't be washed away was her anger. She slowly dressed in a peach and light brown wrap dress – one that flaunted her curves. She wanted to make sure that when she saw Chinelo, there was no mistaking who was in charge of the conversation. Her concealer, light powder, and eyeliner that effectively covered the bags under her eyes finished off her look.

Amara stepped out of her car and walked up to Gozie's house. *I hope this is the place.* She hadn't been to this side of Dallas before, although Chinelo had given her the address some time ago. It was early afternoon, so Chinelo should be the only one at home. Obinna went to summer camp with his cousins and Gozie was a truck driver.

She pressed the bell. No answer. She pressed it again. She noticed the binds shift. Then the door opened.

"Amara..." Chinelo started.

Amara raised her hand to Chinelo's face. "Save it." She brushed past her and stepped into the house. She looked around. Gozie had done well for himself.

Chinelo closed the door and ushered Amara to the couch in silence. Although Chinelo was older, Amara was taller. Chinelo's demeanor made Amara smile inwardly.

Good – she doesn't know what to expect.

Amara opened her mouth to recite the speech she had prepared on the way over, when Chinelo blurted out, "I'm sorry."

Amara was sure shock was written all over her face. If it wasn't, then she was definitely sure her tone would relay the message. "No! You do not get to say that. What? You're sorry? No, ma'am. You don't get to sit there and tell me you're sorry and think we'll kiss and make up." Amara's body shook. She couldn't believe the nerve.

"Amara, *biko*. I don't have any other words to say. I could explain until I'm blue in the face. It won't change anything," Chinelo said.

"What part are you sorry for? For pretending to be my sister and having my back while lusting after my man? Or telling me that if I felt so strongly about calling off the wedding then I should go ahead, knowing you were looking for a chance to slime your way in? Or is it for laughing at me behind my back as I tried to repair whatever was wrong with you and Ejike? Or no, I guess it's for the shock of your betrayal stressing me out so much that I lost my unborn child."

Amara was crying uncontrollably. This wasn't how she intended this talk to go. But she couldn't hold the tears back when she thought of that horrible night when she lost her baby. She didn't want Chinelo to think she was weak, but this was her moment to get it all out. She had lost something that couldn't be replaced by a mere, "I'm sorry."

Amara wiped her face and looked up. Tears rolled down Chinelo face.

"Don't you dare act like you're sorry for me. I don't need your pity." Amara voice was higher than she intended.

"Amara, please just listen to me. I know I don't deserve it. I know you probably hate me, but please hear me out," Chinelo pleaded.

Amara folded her arms and raised one eyebrow. "I didn't listen to Ejike, so there's no way I'm listening to you tell me about that night."

"Please, it's not about that night, but why it happened."

Amara hesitated for a few moments. "This had better be good."

Chinelo lowered her eyes and exhaled loudly, "I'm ashamed to say it, but I've always been envious of you. Don't ask me why, I just have. You seem to have it so together and you're so poised all the time. I had known Ejike forever and he didn't give me the time of day. Then you came along and he was smitten. I was happy for you genuinely, but that night something just came over me. You had called off the wedding. I looked at it as my chance to finally get what was mine."

"But he wasn't yours." Amara brows were scrunched up in disbelief.

"I know that. That's why I kept Obinna a secret all these years. But things started to get hard for me and I was tired and weary. I needed Ejike to take responsibility and to hurt as I was hurting. I was also mad at the fact that you couldn't give him a child and the child he did have was living on the outside. In pain and want." Chinelo paused for a minute then continued. "When I got here, you were still *so* happy despite the pain and misery you must have been going through. I wanted to rock that boat."

"So let me get this straight. Your *waya*, your problem was that I'm happy and you're not? Are you sure you don't need mental evaluation, because you should be committed?" Amara let out a mechanical giggle.

"It might not make any sense to you, but I've just told you what I had going on in my head. I never wanted you to find out this way, truly. Please, I beg of you – forgive. If not for me, then

Obinna. Allow Ejike to be tested as a possible donor for Obinna. *Biko*." Fresh tears rolled down Chinelo's face.

"*E si gini?* What did you say?" Amara asked. "What are you talking about?"

From the way Chinelo's eyes widened, Amara knew she had said something she wasn't supposed to say. Amara stood up and walked behind the chair she had been sitting on.

"What did you say?"

Chinelo went on to tell her about her original reason for coming to America. She had asked Ejike weeks ago to get tested, but he wouldn't do it without Amara on board.

"I gotta go. I just can't with the deceit." Amara hurriedly gathered her keys and purse.

"Amara, please wait. What about Obinna?"

Amara stopped and detected a glimmer of hope in Chinelo eyes. Her eyes narrowed. "Ejike is his own man. You don't need my consent. After all, you didn't get it when you slept with him." Her voice was cold as ice.

She opened the door and walked out. She got into her car and drove off as fast as she could. It wasn't until she had rounded the curve that she pulled over and broke down. This was getting more unbelievable. So the man she thought she loved would rather protect a lie than get a little boy help? Would he have eventually broken down and gotten tested without her? Amara felt like she was having an outer body experience. This surely wasn't her life. It played out like some reality show.

EJIKE DIDN'T THINK it was possible to love a second person at first sight. Seeing Obinna today proved him wrong. At first he had been so nervous, but Chinelo, in her own crooked way, helped him and Obinna to get comfortable. Now that he got that part out of the way, he was trusting God to lead the way with Amara tonight.

Amara was still in bed—curled up in a fetal position—when he left that morning. He didn't know how long this phase would last, but he would give her what she needed. No matter what it was —except a divorce. He just hoped they would be able to talk. He pressed his automatic garage opener and parked his car. He gathered up the roses he bought for Amara.

Ejike opened the door. The living room was in darkness. He raised his hand to the light switch when he saw Amara's packed suitcase in the corner.

"I don't know who you are anymore." Amara's voice was barely audible.

Ejike turned on the light. She was seated on the couch fully dressed. He wanted to speak, but decided to remain silent. He wanted to see where she was going with this. The person sitting before him was totally different from the person he left this morning. Confusion was written all over his face.

"Not only did you keep hidden the fact that you slept with my cousin, but you also you hid the fact that there was a child involved that needed a bone marrow transplant."

He had just gone from the frying pan to the fire. His situation was getting worse. Chinelo must have told her. Ejike was angry. Amara listened to her cousin, but wouldn't give him the chance to explain?

"Where are you going?" He snapped.

"I'm going to my aunt's house in Austin." She fidgeted with her fingers.

"What? When did you decide this? Now hold on a minute." The tone of his voice got her to look up at him. "Babe, please just hold on. You don't even like your aunt that much, so why would you go there? What would you tell her was the reason for your visit?"

She stood. "Ejike—"

"For goodness sake, stop. Hold on. Just stop moving for a minute."

"I can't stay here with you now. I'm about to lose my mind."

"Please, let's talk," Ejike said.

She placed her hands on her hips and started to walk towards him slowly. "What do you think you can possibly have to say to me right now? I don't want to hear it. A trip to Enugu and you fall in bed with Chinelo...my cousin. And subsequently caused this mess." Amara screamed.

She came to a pause in front of him. Tears rolled down her cheeks. Hearing her say it made him hate himself even more. He never intended this to happen and her tears pierced his heart.

"I've tried to stay in this house since we got back from the hospital, but I can't anymore. Since you're here, I'll go. I need to be away from you. I need to think. I need to mourn our child and I'm sure you need to see *yours*." She picked up the suitcase.

"Amara, wait." A beat of silence passed between them, and then he continued, "Amara, you're everything to me. I didn't mean for this to happen. I'd never intentionally do anything to hurt you. I understand you need space right now, so I'll go. I'll stay with Nnamdi for a couple of days."

He dropped the flowers on the side table and went upstairs to pack.

CHAPTER 18

The hours morphed into days. Each day came with its own challenges and emotions. Amara swiped her iPhone screen to reveal the calendar. It had been six weeks since she found out that her husband had fathered a child by her sister-cousin and she had lost hers.

After Ejike moved out, Amara threw herself a pity party that lasted for days. Pity then invited depression and anger to join in on the fun. Sometimes, after watching marathon episodes of Scorned on the ID channel, she found herself daydreaming of hurting them. She wanted to inflict the same pain that they had inflicted on her. She longed for revenge. Those thoughts scared her as they went against everything she believed in. But then again, what did she believe in? Nothing made sense.

As October bowed out to make room for the Thanksgiving month, she decided that her biggest revenge would be to take her life back. She was tired of living like the victim. Gloria Gaynor's, *I Will Survive* played from her phone as she stared into the bathroom mirror. Yes, she would survive with or without Ejike.

She turned her head to examine the small pimple on her left cheek. Her eyes connected with her collection of gospel CDs in the corner. She scoffed. If God could let all this happen to her, she knew she was really alone and had no one looking after her. So, she needed to start doing things her way.

First step was to get back into the full swing of things at work. Tisa had tried to keep up on various requests, but there was only so much she could do. The numerous emails Amara had sent out about the Roberson Kids initiative were finally beginning to gain some attention. During her haze, she still tried to keep things together, especially after getting an email from the One Child Foundation in Atlanta. They wanted Devon to speak at their charity event that was scheduled for this weekend. She had lost a lot of planning time. This was the exposure Devon needed, so she had a lot of work to do. For someone who didn't have a current contract with the NBA, this was pure gold – especially since he had left after his first year. She loved her job and right now it was the only part of her life that made any sense.

Minutes later, Amara was dressed and fed. She started to walk out of the house when she caught her reflection in the mirror. She twisted her lips as she contemplated her attire. She decided to loosen the top button of her maroon and white polka dot blouse to make her gold necklace more visible. She slipped into her maroon heels and placed the blazer to her white pantsuit across her arm. Content with what she saw, she left the house.

Her phone buzzed right as she let down the garage. Amara looked at the caller ID. It was her mom. She probably had another sermon about how a woman should be more forgiving and believing in divine providence. After about a week of separation from Ejike, Amara told her mother about her miscarriage and everything else that was going on. As expected, after empathizing for a while, her mother had said, "Amara, when have you seen me send your father out of the house in thirty years? Even after he married another wife when I couldn't have a son for him, I still stayed. Marriage is about endurance in the good times and bad. If you said he was beating you, *eben*, I'd be the first person to rescue you. But that young man loves you. You have to let go of the pain. Until you do that, you can't forgive."

Amara had spent the next twenty minutes listening to archaic beliefs on marriage.

The phone rang the second time. Amara breathed in, activated her headset, and answered the call. She mentally calculated the five-hour difference.

"Good afternoon, Mummy."

"Afternoon, my love. Are you headed to work?" her mother asked.

"Yes, ma. How is Daddy?"

"Your dad is fine. Worried about you."

"I'm fine, ma."

"Okay, so how is your husband?"

"He should be fine, too. I talked to him yesterday," Amara said. The minute she did, she regretted it. She should have kept quiet, because she had just prepared the podium for another sermon. *Here it comes in five, four, three, two...*

"What do you mean yesterday? Is he not in the house, yet?"

Amara remained silent. She contemplated accidentally disconnecting the call.

"Amara, Amara, Amara, and how many times did I call you?"

"Three times." Amara rolled her eyes. Some things never changed. Her parents, like most Nigerian parents, called their child more than once when they wanted to stress a point, like the first time wasn't enough. Then they had to make the point of asking them how many times they called them.

"Three times *o kwa ya?* Right? Let me draw my ear for you as well. You may think you are all westernized, but unless you don't want your husband, you better let him back home. He made a mistake. From what you said, it was when you foolishly called off the wedding. I'm not condoning his deceitfulness, but you have to open your heart to forgive. It is only when you let go that the healing can begin. As for the miscarriage, the God that wiped my tears and gave me you will wipe your own again. He will give you another child, but you have to free your mind. Allow forgiveness a chance in your home. You're a woman of God and I believe deep down you know I'm right."

Amara was tired of her mother acting like she should just chuck her feelings aside and move on like nothing was wrong.

As though she read her mind, her mom said, "Amara *nwa m,* your name is Amarachi, meaning the grace of God. Whatever comes your way, God's grace will give you the strength to carry it. That is what grace is – that unmerited favor that gives us the desire and the power to do God's will. And what is His will? Love. If you don't forgive, you can't love. It's not easy, but try. I know you love your husband. Remember, I'm your mother and will never lead you astray."

Amara was glad when she saw her office complex in sight. All the energy she had, had been drained with this "Sermon on the Mount" her mother just provided.

"Okay ma, I've heard you. I'll call you later. I'm at work now."

"I know you're trying to get me off the phone, but remember what I see sitting down, you can't see standing up. I don't want you to regret anything."

Amara chuckled. *You should've seen he cheated before the wedding....*"Mummy, I'm not getting rid of you... I really have to go. Love you."

THE CALL from her mother wasn't the only one she got preaching about giving peace a chance. The moment she sat down behind her desk, her cell phone vibrated again. It was Ejike. He had called her every day—morning and night—since he moved to Nnamdi's house. He was his normal caring and loving self, but Amara couldn't get past the fact that he had fathered a child and it wasn't hers.

Amara hadn't spoken to Chinelo since that day she went to see her. The only way she knew Chinelo was still in the country was that Gozie had called and tried to make things right between the ladies.

Amara figured this avoidance and denial strategy wasn't going to fix anything, but right now, she wanted to believe that everything was just a dream.

I can't deal. I can't. She shook her head. She took another sip of her lukewarm second cup of tea. She didn't want to deal with the ugliness. Ejike, of course, was getting impatient. She could tell. He hadn't expected to be away from home this long, but she needed time.

That wasn't the end of it. The next call she got was from First Lady Harris. She let it go to voicemail. This was the sixth week in a row she hadn't been to church or Wednesday Bible study. Amara was certain she'd get a call from the First Lady, and today was the day. Especially since they were about to embark on planning the holiday, "Stretch Out Your Hand" activities. Every year during the holidays, The Way Living Church adopted shelters— especially those with kids. They would feed and buy gifts for Thanksgiving and Christmas. Amara was the co-chair, but right now, she didn't feel like planning anybody else's memorable holiday.

~

A COUPLE OF HOURS LATER, she was back at home. Showered and dressed in her silk pajamas, Amara sat yoga style on the couch and logged on to her Facebook account. She really wasn't a social media person, but had to create a page for her business. She scheduled a few updates for the week while half watching the cooking program, *Chopped.*

Everywhere she turned in the house, something reminded her of Ejike. She missed him, but her heart ached. She needed to get away from here, even if it was just for the weekend. She planned to do just that with this trip to Atlanta.

She'd had a telephone conference with Mr. Roberson that morning. He was excited about the One Child Foundation conference and so was she. They made plans to meet in Atlanta on Friday morning, since his speech would be on Saturday morning. Amara knew she didn't have to go, but she needed the break. She could imagine her mother, hands on her hips, shaking her head in disapproval, but Amara didn't care. This was her life and no one could tell her how she should act or feel.

Throughout the day, thoughts of Ejike and Chinelo flooded her mind and she became angrier. He could have chosen anybody but Chinelo. And then to keep it a secret was just too much for her to bear or forgive. She swiftly flicked away a tear that had rolled down her cheek. No more tears.

The doorbell rang. Amara's eyes darted to the wall clock. It was 8:00pm. She wasn't expecting anybody, especially since she had talked to Ejike already and reiterated to him that she wasn't ready for him to come home yet, if ever. She put on her house slippers and headed to the door. She peered out of the peephole. First Lady Harris. Amara took a breath and opened the door.

"Mrs. Harris, what a surprise," Amara said.

"Sister Amara, God bless you. How are you?"

Amara escorted the pastor's wife into the living room. Mrs. Harris was probably older than her mom. She did a good job mothering the church. What Amara liked most was that she knew everyone by name and seemed to genuinely care.

"Can I get you anything to drink?"

"No, thank you. I won't be staying long." Mrs. Harris eyes roamed around the house like she was looking for something. She had been here once before, when the Dike's invited her and Pastor Harris to bless the house when they first moved in.

"I'm sorry I wasn't able to return your—"

"Hush, child, I know you've been avoiding church and God.

And the reason I know that is because you've been in our church for five years. Served earnestly and at no time have you and your husband been absent for this long. Call me nosy, but Jesus gave my husband authority over His flock so since Pastor can't be here himself, I am. Not to pry, but pray."

Amara couldn't control the tears that streamed down her cheeks. She was speechless. Amara felt Mrs. Harris's arm wrap around her. First Lady began to pray, "Father God, please send down Your peace that surpasses all understanding on your child. Heal her heart from whatever is wrong. You are the All-seeing and All Knowing God. Have your way Lord. In Jesus Name. Amen."

"Amen," Amara whispered.

CHAPTER 19

This was getting ridiculous. Ejike looked at the calendar on his mobile phone. Forty-six days. Forty-six whole days since he had enjoyed the comfort of his own home. He stood up from the full-sized bed he had occupied since he got to Nnamdi's house. He stretched his body and heard his joints crack. His six-feet, four-inch frame was rebelling against being cramped into such a small bed. He had every intention of remedying the situation today.

Freshly showered, he quickly dressed and left the place he temporarily called home. How did his life get this way? He should be waking up beside the warmth of his wife, not in a guest room that had no life in it. Through all the bumps and shakes of their marriage, he and Amara have never spent a day separated from each other. So this felt like a lifetime. He needed her like he needed air. He had agreed to give her space, but she was taking it too far.

He got in his car, connected the headset to his phone and dialed Amara. After three rings with no answer, he hung up and called her office.

"Colab Relations, this is Tisa, how may I help you?" Tisa answered the phone on the first ring.

She sounded so chipper that Ejike was almost envious of her light mood.

"Tisa, how are you? Is Amara there?" he asked.

"Mrs. Dike hasn't made it back, yet."

Ejike looked at his watch. It was 10:00 am. Where could she have gone that she was making it back from? He talked to her the previous night and she didn't mention going anywhere. In fact, she didn't say much at all since it was late and she was seeing off the pastor's wife. That was the second time this week Mrs. Harris had stopped by. Ejike wished he were a fly on the wall. Knowing Amara, she probably wouldn't have disclosed their business to anyone. But then again, she wasn't acting like the Amara he knew, so he took nothing for granted.

"Back?"

"Yes, she went to get a few things for the trip."

Ejike didn't want to alert Tisa that he had no earthly idea of the trip she was talking about, so he told her to tell Amara to call him back.

Ejike couldn't concentrate all day. He couldn't really defend himself when his boss summoned him after they had concluded a crucial meeting that morning.

"I don't know what's been going on with you Dike, but you need to fix it," his boss said.

"I understand. I apologize," Ejike replied. He knew he had no excuse. This was their second biggest client and he had totally messed up.

"An apology is not enough." His boss stood up and walked to the window. "You almost cost the company a huge potential client. You presented another client's numbers to them. That's unacceptable."

Ejike walked out of that meeting with a warning. No second chances. What he had worked so hard for—his promotion—hung in the balance. He blamed his distraction on Amara.

He finally got a call back from her telling him that she was taking a two-day trip to Atlanta. She was changing right before his eyes.

He turned into the driveway of Nnamdi's house. When she came back on Sunday morning, they were going to talk about this once and for all. He had wronged her terribly, but she couldn't just push everything they shared down the drain without a backward glance. She stubbornly refused to talk about anything. Not their loss, Obinna, or Chinelo.

Nnamdi's Mercedes Benz was in the driveway. Ejike hadn't known whether he would be back or not, but he was glad he bought Chinese for two. He was tired of eating Nnamdi's assorted frozen dinners. Using the key his friend had given him, he opened the door, carefully balancing the take-out packs on one arm. Ejike could hear the bass of the surround sound coming from the den. He placed the food on the table and turned the corner to the room Nnamdi called his man cave. Because of the women he entertained from time to time, he didn't want his main living area looking like a total bachelor's pad. According to him, he wanted them to see potential. That line of thought was strange to Ejike, coming from a man who felt marriage was a shackle to the many freedoms God intended man.

When Nnamdi saw him, he picked up the remote to reduce the volume of the movie he was watching. "You're back already?"

"Yes, oh... early day," Ejike replied. After the meeting with his boss, there was no need to stay on for the day. There was no use pretending to be productive. So he decided to call it a day.

"What's good?"

Ejike really didn't know the answer to that question. In his world right now, nothing was good. He should be elated that he had a son, but the circumstances of his birth were not the best. Ejike knew that if it had been someone else, Amara might be more willing to forgive him. More disposed to give their marriage a chance.

"Hmmm, nothing. And that's the honest truth."

"Man, you're wasting time oh...I can't believe that you haven't been able to use your charm to get your wife back," Nnamdi said.

"It's easier said than done. Don't you know what I've done?" Ejike said with his head hung low. And he had indeed tried. He sent her flowers every other day with an apology note. He offered to take her to dinner on numerous occasions. But Amara had shut down all his gestures.

"*Ehen?* You're not the first man and you won't be the last. It's done, so what are you doing to fix it? Because until you do, you'll be in limbo." Nnamdi gulped some water.

Ejike contemplated for a few, and then left the room to get the food he had placed on the table. Returning with bottled water and napkins, he set the food down. He almost laughed out loud at the speed with which Nnamdi ransacked the bags for utensils.

"Well, go ahead then. Help yourself," Ejike said.

The two men ate in silence for a while. Ejike sensed Nnamdi watching him. With his eyebrows raised, he looked behind him. "What? Why are you looking at me like that?"

"I'm just wondering how foolish you can be. You've been the unhappiest I've seen since I've known you. Amara truly loves you. If there was ever a time your adventurous spirit should kick in, it should be now. I thought you liked a challenge. Figure out a way to make her listen to you."

Ejike wiped his mouth with a napkin. "I really love her. I don't know how I could have been so stupid and careless."

"Alcohol can do that to you. But don't forget, you and Amara had called off the wedding."

"That's no excuse and even I know it. The only reason she called it off was because she found out about her infertility and wanted to save me from some unforeseen future deprived of children. God blessed us with a wonderful marriage, successful careers, and finally a child. But then my betrayal was brought to the light, and we lost our child in the process. I'd give anything to turn back the hands of time," Ejike lamented.

"I feel you. But stop whining. Truth is, you can't turn back the hands of time. We make mistakes and have to live with them. My question to you is how do you intend to live with yours? Defeated or a victor?" Nnamdi chuckled.

"Why are you laughing?

"Check me out preaching. The only thing left is to pass the collection plate."

"Nonsense..."

"You see a man is not honored in his home. If this was a church, you'd be writing all kinds of offering checks for that little nugget I just dropped." Nnamdi laughed.

"You see, you were making sense until you decided to clown," Ejike said. "I'll be ready for her when she gets back."

"From where?"

"She'll be going to Atlanta in the morning. Duty calls." Ejike spent the next few minutes filling his friend in on Amara's trip.

"Hmm, she's on a trip with a man. Alone. The same woman who is mad at her husband right now." Nnamdi's disbelief was evident.

"What are you insinuating?"

"You do the math."

"Nnamdi, *abeg*. I trust my wife."

"If you say so."

"I say so. Let me tell you about trust in a relationship, since you seem clueless. A relationship is like sand in your hand. Hold it loosely with respect and its stays. When you close your hand and become possessive, it slips through your fingers. I trust my wife," Ejike took a swig of his bottled water.

"I hear you. Relationship master, the same way she trusted you, *abi?*"

Ejike shook his head. He wouldn't allow those seeds to fester in his mind. Amara was hurt, but wasn't in any way about to look to anyone else for solace. Nnamdi was just talking through the side of his neck again.

"Okay, Okay. Amara isn't like that. But why do you have to wait? Go to Atlanta. You know where she is, right? Neutral ground for both of you. Make it happen. Grovel if you have to, but make her listen and get your woman back. You're beginning to cramp my style—hanging around here moping." Nnamdi clasped his chopsticks together and began to devour the rest of his noodles.

"You're right." Ejike settled back in his chair. He mentally made a plan. He would book his trip to Atlanta for the next morning. He would surprise her when she arrived in Atlanta. Tomorrow, he would make his wife remember what made them so special.

Chapter 20

Amara was awakened by the wake-up service the hotel offered. She stretched out in the bed. The Peachtree Hotel where she decided to stay was perfect. It had a four-star rating and was close to the airport. She reached over to the table by the bed for her iPhone. No missed calls or emails.

So Ejike hadn't even called to make sure she had gotten to Atlanta safely. Well, she didn't want him to call. Or did she? As angry and hurt as she was, she missed her life. Her confidant, her lover, her best friend. She rubbed her stomach. She missed that in the coming months, she wouldn't know what it felt like to have another human growing inside her.

Amara had been researching a lot about miscarriages. Twenty-five percent of all pregnancies ended in the first trimester. To be fair, it wasn't all Ejike's fault. She should've thought about the baby before she bolted out of the house. Amara pushed the "had-I-known's" to the back of her mind. No use pondering that now.

In the next couple of days, away from Dallas, she was going to strategize what to do next. Amara knew that making a little boy suffer for the mistakes of grown-ups was unfair. But she didn't want to see the boy or get to know him. She couldn't bear seeing physical evidence of Ejike's betrayal—an offspring that didn't come from her – his wife. Her skin crawled knowing that Chinelo probably named him Obinna, meaning "like his father," just to spite her.

How could I have been so stupid? The signs were all there. The heart of man is wicked sha. Amara closed her eyes and exhaled. A tear escaped her eyelids. She quickly wiped it away and did a mental shake of her head. She couldn't afford to go there today. She needed to get herself together. This was her first out of town gig for any client and she was determined to be present and available—physically and mentally.

She swung her legs off the bed, inserted her feet into her slippers and walked over to the sink. She rinsed out the coffee pot, filled it, and poured water into the compartment. In a couple of minutes, the room was filled with the soothing aroma of fresh coffee.

She turned on the television and caught a glimpse of *Every Day with Joyce Meyers*. Amara quickly changed the channel. She was not in the mood to listen to anyone preach. Especially not Mama Joyce, as she was fondly called. Amara knew that a forgiveness sermon would be right up her alley. Amara didn't want to forgive and that was that.

Is it by force? That was the reason she had avoided listening to her audio sermons or going to church. She was not in the right frame of mind to be around people, especially those who thought that Christians had to be on a spiritual high all the time. *Well, it ain't happening.*

By noon, Amara pulled into a vacant parking spot near the entrance of the Le Meridian hotel. She pulled down the visor, checked her make-up again, and got out of the car. The color red always made her feel fearless and that's exactly why she opted for the suit she had on. Its skirt stopped right at her knees and the matching, peplum blazer sat perfectly on her hips. Being an emotional wreck on the inside didn't mean it had to show on the outside.

She had talked with Devon. He and his wife, Yvonne, were on their way to the hotel as well. He sounded nervous. She was amazed at how someone whose presence made the room feel small could be so intimidated by public speaking.

She strolled into the hotel. For the middle of the week, the lobby seemed really busy. She passed by a few specialty shops as she followed the signs to the Webcaster Ballroom. The mid-size room was decorated elegantly. Miniature "One Child" logos were placed on each of the rounded tables that could sit about eight people. Apart from the miniature logos, each table had bottles of water and a dish of mints. She spotted her contact, Mr. Lowden. She walked over and they exchanged greetings. He briefed her quickly on the last minute change – Devon had been moved up on the agenda. He now had only twenty-five minutes for his speech and presentation. Mr. Lowden showed her where to hand over the taped recording of the work that Roberson Kids foundation did in Rwanda. She was making her way back to her seat when she heard a voice behind her.

"Amara..." Devon's voice shaky. "I'm so nervous."

Amara turned around to see the Robersons. They were the perfect couple. Yvonne Roberson had a glow about her that for a split second Amara envied. Then she quickly chided herself. That was the same glow she'd had until a few weeks ago when everything came crashing down. This episode had taught her that things were never as they seemed.

"You'll be fine. Trust me," Amara said, smiling. "Yvonne, you look lovely."

"Thanks. You do, too. Red is definitely your color," Yvonne said.

"Why, thank you."

Turning her attention to Devon, Amara went over his speech again. She told him of the change and gave additional pointers on where to stop after emphasizing a point. She rearranged some things so that he could capture the essence of his speech in the first three minutes. She had been taught in school that you had the first couple of minutes to grab the attention of your audience or lose them for good. She always ensured her clients did just that, especially when they gave radio or television interviews.

They spent the remaining minutes before the event kicked off to network. Amara had done her research, so knew the exact people that she needed to introduce him to.

~

THE EVENT WAS A HIT. Amara had gotten a couple of pledges for the foundation and others wanted more material and information after Devon spoke. Coincidentally, the Robersons were staying in the same hotel as she. They had a late night flight back to Dallas, so they all decided to have dinner in one of the hotel's restaurants together.

At first, Amara didn't feel like being around a couple that was obviously in love. She watched the tender exchanges between the Robersons all day. It was a miracle she hadn't burst into tears. She didn't have anything else to do, as the tickets for Sights & Sounds Atlanta Tours were not valid 'til the next day. She had made arrangements to go on the tour on Sunday to see a little bit of Atlanta then head back to Dallas on Monday. At this point, dinner beat staying in the room and crying. She longed for her husband, but that longing turned into anger at what he had allowed their life to become.

"I'll be right back. I need to check in with the nurse and see how dad is doing. Honey, please order for me. I'll be back." Yvonne kissed her husband on the lips and left the table.

"Don't mean to pry, but is your dad sick?" Amara asked.

"Yes, he is. He's staying with us until we can find him a nursing home," Devon replied.

"So sorry to hear that," Amara said.

She lifted her glass to her lips and contemplated for a second. Nursing homes were something that wasn't done back home. It would be a federal case if any Nigerian child suggested that their parent be put in a nursing home because they were ill or getting old. She could just imagine it now. The whole family would gather in an effort to remind you of all the things your parents had done for you and to convince you how much of a bad child you were. The thought brought a smile to her face.

"You're actually smiling. That's good," Devon said.

"I do smile."

"Not in the last couple of times we've met." He paused. "Forgive me for saying this, but I was beginning to wonder what happened to the woman I saw on the first day we met."

"You men can drive a girl up a wall." She shouldn't have said that. Now the man would think she was crazy. She hadn't even told Tonye the real issue so, why was she telling a total stranger her business? Devon was obviously startled by her outburst, so there was an awkward silence between them.

Amara looked around. *Where is Yvonne? How long can one phone call take?*

"I guess I did ask. But that's a general statement. Not all men drive women up a wall. Besides, I can say the same for you women." He folded his hands across his chest and relaxed into his seat.

"Please, forget I said anything."

"What does the good book say? Out of the fullness of the heart the mouth speaks?" He smiled, and then continued. "Besides, a problem shared is half solved, and since I presume you are talking about your husband, you might want a male perspective."

Amara sighed and turned around again. No Yvonne in sight. She lowered her eyes, not able to look at him. "My husband and I are just going through a rough patch."

"I haven't been married long, but I do know that relationships are like bull rides. There will be rough patches along the way. But if you love him—true unconditional love—you hold on for dear life during those rough times and pray you guys come out in one piece in the end."

"How do you know so much about love?" Amara asked. From the outside, Devon didn't look like one who talked about the Bible or wanted to be bound by love.

"I don't. Yvonne taught me. I used to wonder how she stayed with me so long. She would always say, love covers a multitude of sin. When I found Christ, I knew exactly what she meant."

Amara couldn't believe her ears. How funny. She had spent the last weeks running from church and this morning she ran from Mama Joyce, but God still brought a message through a six feet plus, dark and handsome package.

"Wish it was that simple."

"Do you believe he loves you? You don't have to answer. Just think about it. If you believe he does, then he's going through hell as well."

Amara put her head in her hands. What she heard next was more bizarre.

"I could pray with you." Devon must have sensed her hesitation to placing her hands in his outstretched hands. "I don't bite."

She placed her hand in his and he prayed.

After a heartfelt prayer, he said, "In Jesus' name."

"Amen." She stared at him. "I would have never pegged you for the prayerful type."

"Dang it. I thought I wore my 'prayerful type' sign on my forehead today."

Amara flung her head back and laughed. Devon joined in. It felt good to laugh.

"Glad to know you're happy…"

Amara froze. Her insides knotted at the sound of the voice that just spoke. It belonged to her husband.

She slowly lifted her eyes.

Ejike's clenched jaw and fiery eyes told her that he was about to explode. He pulled up a chair and sat down with an exaggerated grin on his face. "I'm sure you guys wouldn't mind if I join your party."

Amara remained speechless. How did he get here and what was he doing here? She opened her mouth to speak, when Ejike continued.

"You must have the magic touch to get my wife to laugh like that." He looked in Devon's direction. "She did tell you she's married, right?"

Devon had a confused look on his face. His eyes travelled from her to Ejike.

"I'd hate for you to go to hell because you drank from another man's well," Ejike said.

Amara had heard enough. Ejike was deliberately being obnoxious and rude. If she didn't do something, he would end up costing her this client.

"Devon Roberson, meet my husband, Ejike Dike." Amara fumed. How dare he act like she was doing something wrong?

"Nice to meet you," Devon extended a hand.

Ejike ignored his hand. "I wish I could say it was a pleasure."

That was it. Amara had had enough. She stood up and looked at Devon. " Excuse us. I'll be back shortly."

Ejike stood. "Don't bother. I'll see myself out." He turned around and left without a backwards glance.

CHAPTER 21

Ejike had no idea where he was going when he busted through the hotel double doors. How could Nnamdi have called it? Amara hadn't so much as turned her lips up in a smile toward him in weeks, and here she was, head thrown back and laughing it up with another man. He gripped his carry-on bag tighter.

"Please, bring my car back around," he said to the valet. It shouldn't take long since he just got here.

Considering the effort it took him to get here, he needed to punch something. He had gone back to the work after speaking with Nnamdi. It took him literally until 8:00 pm to tidy things up at the office. Ejike told his boss that he had urgent family matters to handle out of town before he was let off the hook for the Neoh & Sons project Monday meeting. He had spent hours coaching his replacement for the meeting—something he had dedicated four months to. He had done everything to get down here. When he got to the airport the previous morning, his flight was delayed, then rescheduled, then cancelled. He then decided to get on another airline with a layover. All in an effort to be here so he could work on his marriage. But it was evident that Amara had let it go.

"Ejike Lancelot Dike," Amara screamed.

Ejike was already worked up and she was deliberately trying to make him angrier by calling him by his middle name. He hated that name with a passion and she knew it.

"What?" his voice exploded.

"What is wrong with you? Are you out of your mind?"

"Me? Are you talking to me?" He looked around. She couldn't be talking to him like that.

"Yes, why would you do that to my client?" she asked, hands on her hips.

"Which *yeye* client? Are you that chummy with all your clients?" He watched her mouth open and then close.

"I'm not even going to dignify that question with an answer."

The screech of a car notified him that the valet had returned. Ejike opened the door to put his luggage inside.

"Where do you think you're going?"

"Away from here. I've already done something I'd promised God I wouldn't do again. Lose my temper."

"Ejike, you have to apologize to the Robersons."

"Robersons?"

"Yes, Robersons. He's here with his wife. She stepped away for a minute." Amara folded her arms across her chest. The look on her face confirmed what he knew in his heart. She couldn't have anything to do with another man. He might have just cost her a huge client. Listening to Nnamdi had never paid off.

Ejike had never felt so embarrassed in his life. He was so overtaken by jealousy that he hadn't seen the third place setting. How could he let rage blind him so? No, it wasn't rage, but the fear of losing her to someone else. As a result, he had gravely miscalculated. Now he was going to have to tuck his tail between his legs and apologize. He had made a terrible first impression.

He closed the door, took out his luggage and signaled the valet. With one hand thrust into his pocket and the other on his luggage, he stared at her, then at the hotel.

Amara walked in ahead of him. Her body language told him she wanted nothing to do with him now. At least until he rectified the situation.

Ejike noticed the hard look on Mr. Roberson's face. He was standing at the reception desk near his wife with their bags packed. It was obvious they were checking out. His wife was beautiful, so Ejike imagined that the man should understand how he felt. Ejike knew that justification was lame. He had no excuse.

He walked up, and Amara spoke. "Sorry about that. Ejike, this is Devon and Yvonne Roberson."

Ejike remembered the day Amara told him about her new client some months ago. He could have sworn he wasn't married then.

"I apologize for what happened back there." Ejike extended his hand.

"It's cool. I'd probably have done the same thing considering…" Devon Roberson said, taking his hand.

Ejike wondered what he meant. Did Amara tell him their business? His eyes darted towards her, but she looked away.

"Are you guys ready to leave?" Amara asked.

Mr. Roberson remained silent, but his wife spoke up. "Yes, we'll grab something to eat at the airport. We have to get home because the nurse has to leave tonight."

The receptionist called for his attention and Devon turned to sign some additional papers.

"Okay, we're all set. Thank you so much for everything, Amara. We'll see you back in Dallas."

"No, thank you for everything," Amara said. The women hugged.

"Devon couldn't have done this without you," Yvonne said.

With a nod of acknowledgement, Devon and Yvonne Roberson walked out of the hotel, leaving Ejike and Amara standing there alone.

Ejike could see the daggers in her eyes as she strode off. This was not about to happen again. They were going to talk, even if he had to tie her up. She was going to listen to him.

Chapter 22

The tension in the elevator as they made their way to Amara's room couldn't be cut with a machete, even if they tried.

Amara rubbed her hands on her skirt. *This man is a joker if he thinks he can come in here and act like he's crazy. Did he actually think he had the upper hand here?* If she didn't know better, she would have thought he was on *ogogoro*—a Nigerian, locally brewed, alcoholic drink.

Once inside her room, Amara flung her laptop bag and her purse on the bed and kicked off her shoes.

"Ejike, *ara o na ya gi*? Are you crazy? Do you know what you could have cost me?"

"Amara, I've already apologized for that. Don't make it worse than it is. The man said he understood." Ejike rolled his hand luggage to the corner of the room.

They stared at each other for what seemed like eternity, neither of them breaking their hold on the other. Amara could feel the chemistry they always shared pull her to him. Her body told her that as angry as she might be, she missed her husband. Her body ached for his touch, his warmth. She wanted to cave, but her heart reminded her why it hurt so bad. A betrayal she might be ready to forgive, but it was with Chinelo and they had a son. How could she forgive him? How?

My grace is sufficient for you. The 2 Corinthians 2:19 verse popped into her head. She broke the standoff and walked to the window. All the fight in her seemed to have vanished. All she wanted was for him to leave her alone. She wasn't ready to talk about it.

"Amara—"

"Ejike, I'm tired...

"You have to listen to me, for the sake of our marriage. Just hear me out."

"I've heard all you had to say." She turned her back to him. He quietly walked to her. She couldn't let him touch her. She would go weak. She moved to the sitting area of the room and sat on the chair. Ejike followed and leaned against the writing table.

"Baby, if you think I'm going to let what we have go down the drain just like that, you are sorely mistaken," he said with his hands shoved deeply into his pockets.

"I don't think you have any bargaining power here."

"Yes, I do, because I love you.

"*Ehen? Love o bu onye ebe?*" Amara's sarcasm was evident as she spun the Nigerian phrase equivalent to, "What's love got to do with it?"

"Stop being childish," he said.

"Childish? Childish? You go and have a baby with Chinelo and I'm childish?"

"Okay, hold on. Hold on." There was silence between them for a few moments. Then Ejike continued. "Give me thirty uninterrupted minutes, please."

After a few seconds, she muttered, "You have ten. Go."

Ejike waved his hand back and forth between them. "This right here is my worst nightmare come true. I never meant to hurt you.

Growing up the way I did, my only desire was to make my wife happy. I've spent the past six years doing that to the best of my ability. What happened between Chinelo and I was the result of stupid, stupid mistake."

"Oh, really now?" She rolled her eyes.

"You promised not to interrupt."

"Okay, continue. Although you haven't said anything meaningful." Amara couldn't recognize the voice coming out of her mouth. She didn't know that much venom was in her. But then again, it's not every day you find out your husband is a father to your cousin's child. Her thoughts were interrupted by Ejike's voice.

Amara remained still as Ejike recounted what happened between him and Chinelo that day. She had stopped at her uncle's house in Aba as he had promised to give her a contribution to her wedding. The weather had been so bad that she couldn't return to Lagos until the following afternoon. Now that she remembered it, there was something different in the way Chinelo behaved in the days leading up to the wedding. She suddenly had nothing good to say about Ejike, neither did he have anything good to say about her. *How could I have been so naive not to see the signs?*

"We had just gotten back together. I couldn't form the words, neither did I have the courage to tell you. What would I say to make you understand? What was there to understand?" Ejike bowed his head. He looked tired.

"So, all these years you said nothing about it or a child?"

"I knew nothing of the child and that's the truth..."

"You didn't know then, but Chinelo has been in this country for weeks. Why didn't you tell me? Why did you let me get blindsided?" Amara's voice was barely audible. She began to sob.

Ejike rushed over to her and pulled her close.

She wrapped her arms around his neck. *What am I doing?* She pushed him away and stood.

"You got it wrong. Chinelo didn't tell me until the day you told me you were pregnant. Baby, I couldn't tell you then. I just couldn't."

"So it was okay for me to find out the way I did and lose our baby in the process?"

"I'll live with that regret for the rest of my life, but my plan was to tell you when we got back from the retreat. Things just got out of control."

"*Ehen nu, ife madu me na nzizo ga puta*. Whatever is done in secret must surely come to the light. Or all these years, have you skipped that part of the Bible when you're reading?"

Amara burned with anger at Chinelo, at Ejike, but mostly at herself. She had let her guard down.

"Amara, I want to come home. We can work this out, together. Please."

"What home?" She scoffed. "*Kai*, that's the same place I left you and Chinelo alone that weekend."

"Whatever you're thinking, stop it. I've not had anything to do with that woman."

Neither of them spoke for a while.

Ejike grabbed his luggage and began walk to the door, his shoulders slumped. Amara recalled Devon's words from earlier. Ejike did look like he was suffering. She wanted to reach out to him, but her unquenched anger wouldn't let her. He got to the door and placed his hand on the knob.

"Wait." Amara didn't know when the word escaped her lips.

Ejike turned around. She could feel his gaze burn through her body. His stare made her shift uncomfortably. His stride was swift as he made his way to her. He wrapped his arms around her. The floodgate of tears she had tried to keep sealed opened and her tears flowed freely. This time her sobs were not driven by anger and hurt, but by surrender and fatigue. Her body relaxed as Ejike pulled her closer to him.

They'd always been a perfect fit. His lips found hers and the kiss that started off slow and sensual grew into one of hunger and need. She needed him just as much as she could feel he needed her. She pulled back.

"Please, forgive me. Let's start over." His plea was desperate.

Amara remained silent for a few minutes. Then she looked up at him. "This changes everything. The way I look at you, our marriage...everything."

"I'd do anything to change that. I'm so sorry," Ejike took both her hands in his.

"We have to go for counseling."

Ejike hesitated. She raised her eyebrow.

"Agreed. I want to come home." He brushed his lips against hers. "I want to wake up every day of my life with you by my side."

"I have to learn to let go. My spirit has been bound by resentment and can only be unbound when I let go," she said between sniffles. "My brain knows that, but I've got to open my heart to catch up."

"Thank you. All I beg of you is that you try." He kissed her forehead.

Amara knew they had a lot to talk about, but she also had needs and one of them was her husband. Now. Their kiss deepened. In one swift motion, he picked her up headed towards the bed.

A couple of hours later, Ejike gently combed his fingers through her hair. She laid her head on his chest. Snugly tucked into his side, she wished she could turn back the hands of time. Despite the safety she felt in his arms, she couldn't ignore the issues that stood between them and had literally changed their lives.

As though reading her mind, Ejike whispered. "Again, I regret the pain I caused you. I should have trusted God to help me fix whatever the consequences would have been then."

"I never would have imagined Chinelo would do something

like this. I always knew she wanted you for herself, but this is even beneath her."

"Baby, all I know is that she needs Jesus if she thought a child would make me leave you for her," he said.

Amara sat up. Her mood was pensive. "She says the boy needs a transplant."

"Yes, but I couldn't do what she wanted without telling you first."

Amara rubbed her stomach and exhaled deeply.

"Baby, I can't say how sorry I am, but nothing, and I mean nothing, means more to me than you." Ejike paused. "We can always have another child. Our success this time around proved that we can. Please give us a chance."

Amara didn't want to consider that possibility now. "So what do you plan to do about Chinelo and Obinna?"

Ejike's eyebrow rose. "I have *no* plans for Chinelo. But I can't abandon the boy—my son."

There was an uncomfortable silence, until Amara broke it. "I know how you grew up, so I won't ask you to. But saying it's going to be a walk in the park because I'm a Christian would be like making a piecrust promise. It would be easily broken."

"Baby, as long as you're willing to give us a chance, we can get through this together."

"I listened to every message you left me over the last five weeks and I know this isn't easy for you as well, but I don't want to see Chinelo again. I know she'll be in your life because of the boy, err I mean Obinna, but keep her away from me." Amara said. To her ears, that didn't even sound right, because as long as there was Obinna, Chinelo would always be in the corner. *I love my husband. Help me get through this, God.*

"Baby, your willingness to try is more than I can ask for. This is not your mess, its mine." He pulled her close. "I love you and have missed you more than you can imagine."

"Oh, yeah?"

"Yeah," he whispered into her neck.

"How much?"

"Showing you will be more effective than telling you." His lips covered hers.

Amara knew she wasn't fully there yet, but with the grace of God, her marriage would weather out this storm.

CHAPTER 23

Ejike pulled his Range Rover into his parking spot. He turned off the engine and tried to figure out his next move. He and Amara hadn't discussed Obinna since they had gotten back last Tuesday. He wanted her to get to know his son. It had been a nerve wracking ordeal in itself to get Chinelo to agree to Obinna spending the weekend with them. She was adamant that Amara would harm her child. Now that she had agreed, all he had to do was to get Amara to consent.

He muttered a quick prayer and got out of the car. "Father, please give me the right words to say. I'm trying to make this right."

The aroma of *egusi* soup teased his nostrils the minute he got into the house. His wife knew how to throw down. He headed into the kitchen and wrapped his arms around her. She was stirring something in the pot.

Ejike snaked his arms around her waist and kissed the nape of her neck. Amara turned around and lightly brushed her lips against his. They shared light banter about their day and then Ejike headed upstairs to get changed.

Later that evening, they were relaxed on the couch. Ejike

watched the news as he gave his wife a foot rub. He loved the way she moaned when he hit a spot, while engrossed in the book on her Kindle. She looked so peaceful and he didn't want to disturb that, but he needed to do this.

"Amara, we need to talk about Obinna," he blurted out. He felt her body tense.

She slowly set down her Kindle and sat up. "Oh, is he okay?"

"Yes, he's fine. I want him to come and spend some time here." He waited for her reaction. Her face provided him no clues as to what she was thinking.

"I don't expect you to bend over backwards for him, but I'd like us to get to know him. Together."

Amara still remained silent, her head bent as though in prayer. Then she raised her head and spoke, "Ejike as unreal as this situation is, it has become my reality. I've not fully processed it, but I've at least begun to live with it. No matter how much I or we try to skip around it, Obinna is a part of you. And I want you, so I'm going to have to find a way to deal with this."

"Again, I'm so sorry. I don't know what I've done to deserve you, but I thank God for you every day."

"Stop apologizing. You mean everything to me as well. Most *Naija* men would have chosen a son over a woman who can't give him a child. And we both know that's the truth."

"Baby, I'd never do that."

"And that's what makes me one lucky woman. Chinelo can scheme all she wants to, but I refuse to give her any more power. I am Mrs. Dike." She waited, and then continued, "No matter how bitter the pill was to swallow, that child needs you. He didn't ask for this, so there should be no reason he should suffer for it."

Ejike looked at her in total awe. He had a whole speech planned out. Bible verses that he would have quoted to the resistance he envisaged she'd put up. But here he was, totally thrown off balance by her unexpected speech.

"Honey, he can spend the weekend with us. Tomorrow is

Friday. Bring him over. I'll prepare the guest room." She picked up her Kindle and started reading again. She must have felt his shock, because after a few moments she asked, "*O gini*? What is it?"

Ejike couldn't respond verbally. She had blown him out of the water. He pulled her close and just held on, and thanked the Holy Spirit for His intervention.

~

As the minutes ticked away, Amara's level of anxiety increased. She looked at the clock that hung on the wall. It was almost lunch time. She left work at noon and had the house ready for when Ejike brought his Obinna home. A part of her was excited that finally she would be able to take care of someone else, but there was also that little voice that kept reminding her of the circumstance surrounding his birth. Ejike had shown her a picture of the little boy. He did have Ejike's dimples. They seemed to be a Dike family trait because Amara remembered some of Ejike's other family members had them, too.

That morning, her husband continued to look at her as if she had grown an extra neck. She knew he wasn't expecting what she'd said last night. She wasn't expecting it either, but she couldn't stop herself once she got going. If the situation wasn't so serious, she would have busted out laughing at the way he remained speechless.

Hmm, maybe I should apply that approach often. He wouldn't know what to expect. She smiled at her genius idea. Her musing was cut short when her phone rang.

"Hello, Mummy. Good afternoon." Amara knew exactly what this conversation would entail. She smiled wondering how long it would take her mother to get to the reason for the call.

"Afternoon *nwa m*," her mother returned her greeting.

"How's daddy doing?"

"Your daddy is fine. *Ehen*, let me ask you...are you prepared?"

That didn't take long. Amara wanted to stall, but then she

knew her mother would lament about the "credit" she had loaded into the phone to make this call.

She couldn't resist. "For what? The second coming? I try to be ready every day." Amara tried to hold her laughter, but a tiny giggle escaped.

"Oh, you are now Ali Baba's apprentice? *O kwa ya?*" her mother asked, referring to Nigeria's number one comedian.

"Don't you see me on stage with him?

"Amara, *bia zam okwu.* Answer me before my credit finishes. Are you ready for your husband's son's visit?"

"Mummy, I'm as ready as I can be. I don't know why you are acting so panicky."

"It's because I know how you ladies of nowadays are."

"And how are we?"

"You don't have patience and the tolerance that is needed for a good lasting marriage."

"Mama, not this again. I'm trying to work on my marriage and to forgive my husband, but I won't have his crime diminished in the name of tolerance. After all, didn't Christ say that adultery was a reason for divorce?"

"You were not yet committed to each other. Isn't that the story you told me? Ejike is a good man and I'm glad you are trying. God will reward you. Just remember, when you get riled up – because you will – the boy is an innocent party in this scenario."

"Okay ma, I've heard you." Amara was eager to change the subject. She was not about to argue with her mother on what commitment meant to her. They spent the remaining time discussing the August Meeting coming up. Amara was always amazed at how this meeting seemed like an end of year party of sorts for Igbo church women. They planned all the festivities up to and including the shoes and the wrappers they would wear that day.

Hours later, Amara looked around the guest bedroom again. She had it fixed up with a Buzz Light Year theme. She thought the

Toy Story character would be appealing to Obinna. She wanted to buy some toys, but Ejike suggested they do that together the next day. That would just be one of the many stops they had planned for the day. When they talked earlier, Ejike hinted that Obinna liked hamburgers, so she'd stopped at the store to buy some minced meat and made some homemade patties that Ejike would grill when they got here. The weather was perfect, so she planned for them to have dinner on the patio.

Hearing the key turning in the lock alerted her that Ejike had arrived. She checked her appearance again.

Her heart began beating faster than ever before, as she made her way down the stairs. She stopped when she saw them. The resemblance between Obinna and Ejike was uncanny. There was no denying that they were father and son. Her anxiety turned to ache as she continued to stare at the boy. His big, brown eyes stared back as she saw a confused look set in.

Ejike must have noticed her discomfort and spoke. "Hi, babe."

Amara continued her descent down the stairs. When she got to the last step, she managed to relax the lines in her face.

"Hey," she said.

Ejike kissed her on the cheek and turned to the little boy. He was dressed smartly.

Well that's one thing his mother knows how to do well. Amara chided herself immediately. If she started this way, the weekend would go downhill from here. She had to at least try. She squatted to meet him at eye level.

"And you must be Obinna?" She smiled, trying to put him at ease.

He nodded his head nervously. It couldn't be easy for him either, having to spend the weekend away from his mother with two complete strangers. Ejike told her that Chinelo had finally agreed to tell the child that he was his father and not Afam as he had believed all these years.

"Obinna, remember I told you that you'll be spending the weekend with me and my wife?" Ejike said.

Obinna remained silent but nodded.

"This is my wife. Her name is Amara."

"Just call me Auntie Amara." Amara didn't want him to be confused on how to address her since he already had a mother. Beside the "auntie and uncle" culture should be familiar to him as that was how any Nigerian child prefixed the name of any older woman or man. Blood relative or not.

"Are you hungry? We're having burgers." Amara got a smile out of that announcement. "A little birdie told me you like burgers. Come, let me show you to your room, then we'll get ready for dinner." Amara noticed him turn to Ejike for some kind of sign it was okay for him to follow her.

"Go on, Obi. Let me get the grill going, then you can come help. You like that?"

"Yes," Obinna spoke for the first time and put his hand in Amara's outstretched hand.

Amara could feel Ejike's eyes burn her back as she climbed the stairs. She couldn't turn to look at him. The physical evidence of his betrayal hurt, but she had promised to be strong and by the grace of God, she knew she could do this.

CHAPTER 24

Amara and Obinna came downstairs. Obinna had changed into some more comfortable clothes and had exchanged his shoes for crew socks. Amara prepared baked beans and a side of coleslaw, while Ejike and Obinna worked on the grill.

Ejike flipped a sizzling burger and studied his wife. He kept cutting glances at her, waiting for a sign that she might be angry or some kind of emotion, but none came. She hadn't made eye contact with him and he was worried. He needed to get her alone to make sure she was okay, but he didn't want Obinna to feel left out.

A short while later, the threesome sat at the table and held hands as Ejike blessed the food. Amara helped Obinna cut his hamburger into quarters so it was manageable.

Finally, she looked at Ejike. Her eyes told him that she was tired and was trying to keep up a brave front. He wanted to hold her and reassure her that everything would be okay.

As the meal went on, the conversation at the table was light-hearted as they tried to get to know more about Obinna—his likes and dislikes. As he spoke, Ejike noticed that behind all the pain, there was a sparkle in Amara's eyes. She would make a great mother. As soon as the time was right, he would talk to her again about them trying to have a baby. He still had nightmares of the evening of her miscarriage and would never forgive himself for it.

By the time dinner was over, they had the next day all planned out. Amara took Obinna upstairs to give him a bath while Ejike cleaned up the kitchen. A few minutes later, he was wiping his hands when his phone rang. The caller's name displayed on the screen brought a frown to his face. It was Chinelo. She had caused so much unnecessary ruckus when he went to get Obinna that he wished he took Nnamdi up on his offer to escort him to her house.

"Hello." He answered the call after the third ring.

"Ejike, how is my son doing?" Chinelo asked. From her tone, it was clear that her attitude hadn't changed since he left her.

He walked into the living room. "Chinelo, our son is fine. I won't harm him."

"It's not you I'm worried about, but that your *"rightchor,"* Chinelo said.

Ejike almost chuckled when Chinelo mentioned the word *right-chor*. He hadn't heard the Nigerian slang for the word, "right-eous" in ages. The reason for her attitude was still foreign to him. He knew that she and Amara had talked a while back. Although nothing was resolved, Amara told him that Chinelo was remorseful. Did she change her mind? What was the issue now?

"Okay, so what's the problem? That Amara hasn't done what you expected. Shown out?"

"Whatever. I don't know what you're talking about."

"Yes, you do. So is it *vexing* you that she has decided to give our marriage a second chance despite your efforts?" He didn't really expect an honest answer.

"She had no other choice. No other man would want her," Chinelo said.

"Chinelo, if you don't want anything else, then let me enjoy this time with my wife and son. I'll bring him back to you on Sunday as promised. You can count the hairs on his head if you want to, then," Ejike said impatiently. He didn't want Amara to hear him on the phone with Chinelo. That would make the tense situation even worse.

There was silence for a few moments.

"Hello?" His tone dared her to ask to speak to Obinna. They had agreed she would make this as easy for Obinna as possible and keep away until Sunday afternoon.

"Yes, I'm here."

"Do you need anything else?"

"I guess not. I'll call again tomorrow after I return from my road trip with my girlfriend to check on him."

"Suit yourself." He disconnected the call.

Ejike knew he should be more patient. Chinelo was just looking for attention. Then again, she wasn't the type of person you let down your guard down with. He had made that mistake once.

AMARA TURNED AROUND and bumped right into her husband's broad chest. He wrapped his arms around her to steady her from falling and then led her out of the room. Obinna was hugged up on a fluffy monkey and looked so peaceful in the full-sized bed. Amara had lined extra pillows around the side of the bed that was away from the wall in case Obinna was a roller.

"How long have you been standing there?" she asked as they walked to their bedroom down the hall. Amara plopped down on the chair next to the window of their bedroom. She was exhausted, mentally and physically. She needed a long soak in the tub.

"Long enough." Ejike left the door slightly open and walked over and began massaging her shoulders.

Amara moaned. She often told him he had the magic touch. His hands were so strong and his fingers applied the right amount of pressure to her aching muscles.

"Babe, thank you," Ejike said.

"You're welcome." There were no additional words necessary. At least not tonight. She didn't want to talk. She couldn't handle any thinking. All she wanted to do now was bathe and relax. It was just 8:30pm. If she slept now, she was bound to wake up before dawn.

"He's a very well-mannered boy."

"Yes, he is. Thank you for being so accommodating." Ejike bent down and gave his wife a kiss on her forehead. "Now, come on. Let me take care of you."

"Hmm, what do you have in mind?" She snickered.

"Get your mind out the gutter, woman."

"See this one, as if you weren't thinking it." She laughed.

"I don't know what you're talking about. I wanted to run you a bath and make you a nice warm cup of tea." He smiled.

"*Ezi okwu.* Yeah, right...Mr. Loverboy." She teased him.

They both laughed. Ejike took her hand and guided her to the bathroom. Amara sat on the closed commode as he turned on the faucet. As the bathtub began to fill, Ejike pulled her up. In silence, he tugged her blouse over her head and began to undress her. He paused after a minute and wiggled his finger under the running water to ensure the right temperature. Then he poured some of her favorite aromatherapy oil into the tub and handed her a shower cap.

"Okay, my love. Get in and I'll be right back."

"Hurry," she said as he walked out of the room.

THE NEXT MORNING Amara was preparing a breakfast of scrambled eggs, sausages, grits and toast when she heard Ejike come down the stairs with Obinna in tow.

"Auntie Amara, good morning," the five year-old said, still groggy.

"Good morning Obi. How are you?"

"Fine."

"Did you sleep well?" Amara asked.

"Yes," Obinna nodded.

"Are you hungry?" she asked.

"Yes."

Amara looked up at Ejike and they both smiled at the boy's monosyllabic responses. "Honey, good morning,"

"Morning, babe. You didn't wake me up," he said.

"How could I? You were sleeping so peacefully." Amara winked at him.

Last night, he did return soon enough, as promised, with a steaming cup of Tetley tea. He left her to soak in solitude, returning only after he thought she had fallen asleep in the bathtub. He dried her off and applied lotion to her entire body before jumping in the shower. After that, he showed her exactly why they were made for each other. His tenderness reminded her of when they first got married.

Why did it always take something so devastating to remind couples to keep the romance alive? She wasn't exempt herself. She had been so preoccupied with having a baby and her career that she had forgotten to enjoy her marriage and her husband. Ejike was changing that and she vowed to do the same.

She watched as Obinna stared at his bowl of grits. He hadn't touched the spoon.

"You don't like grits?" Ejike asked. "I don't blame you. I didn't like them either at first. They had to grow on me."

Obinna wrinkled his nose. "I want cereal."

"Okay, let Auntie check. I might have some." Amara got up from the table and began searching the cabinet for the box of Fruit Loops. She found it and poured some in a bowl and took it to the table.

Obinna's face lit up. He hurriedly grabbed his spoon.

"What do you say?" Ejike asked calmly.

"Thank you, Auntie."

"That's a good boy. You always say, 'please' when you want something and, 'thank you' when you get it." Ejike ruffled Obinna's head lovingly.

"Okay."

~

THE REST of the day went by like the speed of lightning. They had gone to the zoo and explored the Aquarium. They had lunch before ending the day with a trip to the toy store. As they drove home, Obinna passed out in the back seat.

The next morning, Amara, Ejike and Obinna walked into The Way Living Church hand in hand. They made their way to their seats amidst stares and questioning eyes. Mrs. Harris sent her a reassuring smile when their eyes met. Tonye—who had just returned with her husband from celebrating their fifth wedding anniversary in Trinidad—wanted to know if Obinna was the reason for the rumors going around the church about them. Amara, not wanting to rehash the whole saga, reassured her that things were under control. The look Tonye gave her told her she didn't buy it, but something distracted her, so she didn't push it.

"So, in conclusion..." Pastor Harris's voice brought her out of her reverie. Amara didn't realize she had been daydreaming for most of the service. Thoughts of everything that had happened with Chinelo's news, losing her baby, almost losing her marriage, regaining her marriage and then developing a relationship with Obinna had flooded her mind and she hadn't paid a bit of attention. She sat up in her seat to catch the last little bit of the sermon.

"As Christians, we are called to be followers of Christ which means to walk in His ways. His commands like, 'love your neighbor as yourself.' 'If anyone slaps you, turn the other cheek.' 'Forgive those who have offended you seventy times seven times' and the list goes on and on. These are tall orders for ordinary human beings, but once you've become born again and filled with the Holy Spirit, all you need do is call upon Him to help you. With His death on the Cross, Jesus wiped the slate clean for us and reconciled us to the Father. As humans, it's so hard for us to extend the courtesy to others, but think about it this way – forgiveness is crucial for our own prayers to be answered. By holding on to hurt and not being willing to let go, you then block your own blessings. The Christian walk is not an easy one, but it's doable through Christ because of grace. The Bible tells us that His grace is sufficient and made perfect in our weakness."

There was silence from the congregation.

Then Pastor Harris said, "If all else fails and you can't forgive them because you don't think they deserve it, then forgive them because you deserve peace. Forgiveness is not about them, but you."

There was laughter throughout the congregation.

The service wrapped up soon after with the benediction. Amara went to pick up Obinna from Sunday school. On her way, she narrowly escaped Tonye's questioning eyes as she led the new church members into a room behind the sanctuary. Amara smiled as Tonye gestured for her to expect a call after.

"Did you enjoy Sunday School?" Amara asked as she and Obinna made their way to the parking lot.

"Yes, I even have a memo...memo...uhm," Obinna said.

"Memory verse," Amara said with a smile.

"Yes, here." He handed her a small piece of paper with the words, *"And now these three remain, faith, hope and love but the greatest of these is love. ~*1 Corinthians 13:13

A wave of emotion washed over her. In one swift motion, she picked Obinna up and hugged him tight. Without hesitation, he wrapped his small arms around her neck. They were still in that position when Ejike came rushing toward them. She saw the concerned look in his eyes.

Amara put Obinna down. "*O gini*? What is it?"

Ejike looked down at Obinna and smiled a nervous smile. Amara searched his eyes for some kind of answer, but understood that whatever it was, he didn't want to say it in front of Obinna.

On the drive back home, Ejike told Amara that Chinelo had sent him a text telling him that she wouldn't be able to pick up Obinna later that day. Amara kept her cool, deciding not to discuss it with Obinna in such close proximity. She looked at him in the back seat of the car, occupied with his toys. Not a care in the world. And that was how it was going to stay.

Some minutes later, Amara and Ejike were upstairs changing out of their Sunday best.

"I can't believe how selfish Chinelo can be," Amara said.

Ejike kicked off his shoes. "I can."

"So she just up and decided to go with this friend to Vegas? Just like that?"

"That's what the text said. She said she needed time to enjoy herself a little for a change. 'I'm stressed and I'm tired,' were her exact words." Ejike made quotation marks in the air.

Amara dusted her hands off and shook her head.

"This is not good at all. You have to go to Michigan tomorrow," Amara said.

Ejike put his head in his hands. A few moments later, he raised his head and sighed.

"Okay, please get him ready. We'll take him to Gozie's," Ejike said.

Amara huffed. Chinelo was out of this world.

CHAPTER 25

Hours later, Ejike swung his Range Rover into his driveway. He wasn't ready to go inside just yet. The trip to Gozie's house was futile. Gozie couldn't take Obinna because his wife and kids were in New Jersey visiting her family and this was his week to be on the road.

While Obinna slept in the back seat, a million thoughts ran through Ejike's mind. He tried to call Chinelo again, for the umpteenth time. No response. Ejike didn't know how he was going to get Amara to agree to take care of Obinna for some additional days. She had been a gem this weekend, but he didn't want to push it. Suggesting that might have him back in the doghouse. But then he probably wasn't giving her enough credit. She just might surprise him. She had been doing a lot of that lately.

Ejike walked into the house quietly. The blender was going in the kitchen so Amara didn't hear him. Once Obinna was comfortably tucked in upstairs, Ejike made his way back downstairs.

Amara was dicing up onions with a large kitchen knife.

Hmm, maybe I should wait 'til she's done with that knife.

"You're back? I didn't hear you come in. So have you dropped him off?" She picked up the cutting board and poured the onion rings into the sizzling oil.

Good, she's dropped the knife. He opened his mouth to speak, when Amara picked up the knife and began chopping tiny peppers.

Ha! Pepper and a knife. I'll give her a few more seconds.

When he didn't answer immediately, she flung her head up from what she was doing.

"Babe, he's upstairs."

Amara paused and continued cutting up the pepper. Her pace had decreased. "Why? Wasn't Gozie home?"

"He was, but he heads out tonight and his family is in Jersey."

"So what are *you* going to do?" She scooped the peppers into a bowl.

Ejike remained silent.

"*Mba nu nu*...it can't be. You want me to take care of Obinna for the next week or until whenever Chinelo decides to come back?" She pointed the knife toward him.

Ejike walked over, his steps laced with caution. He took the knife from her hand. "Babe, I really, really need this favor."

"I see you want to send me to prison."

"How?" Ejike asked, puzzled.

"Suppose he's allergic to something? Or Chinelo comes back before you and I'm forced to confront her again?"

"Come on, that wouldn't happen. I wouldn't have asked if I didn't really need it and know you could work from home. You're a natural. You took great care of him this weekend." Ejike pleaded his case and hoped it would work.

Amara remained silent.

"You know this is the last leg of this project. And I've been working on it for months."

"I don't want to jeopardize that. But I don't know if I can do this." Amara poured some of the pepper in the oil followed by a blended puree.

"*Biko*...please."
"You would owe me big time."
"No, *wahala*. Thank you."

Amara picked up the Huggy Monkey from the floor. Just a few hours ago, her once serene living room had been turned into a playroom for a five year-old. She climbed the stairs to place the stuffed animal in Obinna's bed. He loved the huggable monkey. He had been so tired from play that he didn't remember it when he went to sleep. She knew he would wake up looking for it, so decided to save him the trouble.

Today was the third day she had been left to care for Obinna. Their routine consisted of a morning bath, breakfast, cartoon and play time. When he watched TV, she checked her emails and caught up on work. When he went down for a nap after lunch, she made important phone calls. At night, he snuggled up against her while she read him a story. Amara watched in amusement every night as he selected a book from the pile she and Ejike had gotten for him.

She had begun to love the little boy. But she couldn't help but wonder how she got here. She had gone from being the victim of a devastating betrayal to taking care of the product of that deceit. Chinelo was still missing in action. She didn't disclose when she would be back, just that she needed to breathe a little. Amara couldn't imagine what it was like to have to care for a sick son, but she still wouldn't have left hers to go "breathe."

Since being with them, Obinna hadn't shown any signs of fatigue or pain, which were the symptoms of an episode. The minute she agreed to care for him, Google became Amara's second home. She needed to familiarize herself with the disorder in case anything happened.

As much as she wanted to resent the situation, Obinna was so adorable that each minute spent with him made her look past how he got here. She could really see him as her own, at least for her husband's sake. To be honest, for her sake, too. She longed to have a child to hold and call hers. If God didn't have it in His will for her to have one naturally, she would make do with the one He had brought into her life.

Amara peered into his room. Obinna was fast asleep. She adjusted the covers he had flung into the corner. She shut the door and walked down the hall to her bedroom. Luckily, she didn't have a lot of emails to respond to or send out. She made up her mind to take a much needed shower and do a little reading while she waited for Ejike to call. He was supposed to call the minute he got out of the meeting he had to attend.

An hour later, Amara had showered and was sipping on some tea when the call she had been expecting came through.

"Hi, honey," she greeted, excitedly.

"*Kedu?* How are you?"

"Tired."

"Hope he didn't wear you out too much."

"What do you think?" She smiled.

"I owe you..."

"Don't worry. I intend to collect my payment in cash and in kind."

The couple laughed and spent the remaining minutes rehashing their day. His meeting had gone according to plan and he would leave Michigan tomorrow afternoon. With the plans of what they'd do when he got back in place, they said a quick prayer together before hanging up the phone.

"AUNTIE AMARA...AUNTIE AMARA," Obinna cried later that night.

Amara thought she was dreaming. She was being nudged, but

it somehow didn't feel like a dream when the hands started to pat her. Her eyes flung open and she shot up to a sitting position. Her eyes darted to the clock on the dresser. It was 2:15am. Obinna was at the side of the bed, tears in his eyes. She picked him up. He was warm. Amara panicked.

"Jesus, please help me. Don't let anything happen to this boy in my hand. No one will believe my story," Amara muttered. "Obi, what's wrong?"

"I don't feel good." He laid his head on her chest. Amara hugged him close.

Okay, be calm. She remembered when she was a kid and ran a temperature, her mother would pat her down with a cold cloth. It helped soothe her. She laid him on the bed. Her first thought was to take his temperature, but she didn't have a thermometer in this house. No reason to. But she was grateful for that little voice that had told her to buy kids Tylenol. She placed him on the bed and went into the bathroom. She returned a few minutes later with a damp cloth and the medicine.

Amara spent the next few minutes wiping Obinna down after giving him the medication. His temperature seemed to go down and he was calmly sleeping. Amara was too scared to take him back to his room, so she let him sleep in hers.

The next morning Obinna refused to eat anything Amara offered. He wasn't as warm as the previous night, but he still had a fever. She didn't want to alarm Ejike, neither did she want to give Chinelo something to talk about, so she didn't call either of them.

I can do this. With determination, she picked up the phone and dialed the only person she knew that could help in this situation.

After the third ring, the phone connected. "Hello," she said.

"Amara, how are you? I thought you had forgotten about me," Nnamdi teased.

"Nnamdi, I'm fine. I can't believe you, though. You knew about all my drama and you didn't even pick up the phone to call me."

"*No be like dat*. It's not like that. What did you want me to say now?"

"Anyway, you and I will settle later. I'm in trouble."

"*O gini?* What is it?"

Amara quickly filled him in on the happenings since yesterday night.

"Okay, bring him into my office. Let's see what's going on. I'll meet you there in about thirty minutes."

By the time Amara arrived at Nnamdi's downtown office, things had gone from bad to worse. Obinna was in the back seat of the car moaning in pain. She swiftly freed him from his booster seat and headed inside the office. Nnamdi must have told the nurses to expect her, because she was immediately taken into a back room. Obinna continued to moan, seated on her lap. Amara was alarmed at the rate at which his temperature rose. A nurse came in a short while later and took his temperature. Amara watched her shake her head.

"Let me go get the doctor. This child needs to be taken to the hospital." She exited the office.

Nnamdi entered the room. "*Nne kedu?*" He greeted her.

"*O din mna jare*. I'm fine. The nurse said we needed to go to the hospital."

Nnamdi proceeded to examine Obinna in silence. He looked up at Amara. "He has a high fever. I can give him something to bring it down, but he does need to go to the hospital."

"Is he that bad? He was fine." Amara's tone hinted alarm.

"Amara, it's common with patients with his blood disorder. They need to test his blood count to see what's going on."

"I have no idea where he is being treated...ha! *Chineke m*. My God."

"Try and get in touch with Chinelo. I'll make a few calls." Nnamdi left the room.

~

AMARA DREADED TELLING Chinelo something was wrong. But she really needed her to pick up her phone right now. Amara threw her phone on the passenger's seat after trying Chinelo again with no response. She hadn't had much luck with Ejike either. He was probably in flight. She peered through the rearview mirror. Obinna was no longer moaning, but she could tell he was restless.

Amara followed closely behind as Nnamdi carried Obinna into the hospital. After she thought about it some more, she had remembered Chinelo telling her that Obinna was being treated at the Wellness Hospital. It didn't take long before Nnamdi found his hematologist. Nnamdi handed the boy to the nurse in the ER who quickly moved into action.

Amara's chest ached. She felt helpless as she watched the nurse and Nnamdi disappear with Obinna through the double doors. She had paperwork to fill out at the reception desk.

Amara sat down with the clipboard. She stared at the form and began to fill it in. *Father's name: Ejike Dike. Mother's Name: Chinelo Edozie. Date of birth*, her hand began to shake. Tears steadily streamed down her cheeks. The past few months flashed before her eyes. She wiped her tears, clearing her blurred vision.

Stop being selfish, Amara. Obinna had nothing to do with this. He's going through enough as it is. Focus on him.

Amara's cell phone rang. She let out a sigh of relief when she looked at the caller ID. It was Ejike. He must have landed. Amara set the clipboard aside.

"Have you landed?" Amara bypassed her normal greeting. Right now, she wasn't in the mood for common pleasantries. Ejike had gotten them into this mess. Even though the baby she lost was just weeks old, to her it was still a child. Now she cared for another child who was seriously ill. She couldn't lose another child.

"Yes, we're still on the runway and I just got your message. Is Obinna okay?"

"No." Amara began to cry again. She rushed through the happenings of the past twelve hours.

"I'll be right there," he said.

"Drive carefully, but please hurry. They want to do some tests on him, but need a parent." She paused. Ejike was silent. "And I can't get a hold of Chinelo."

Amara knew that Ejike's silence meant he didn't know what to say. The weight of her words had cracked a dent into their fantasy world. The world they had created over the past several weeks. A world in which they had tried to forget the issues that had formed a gulf in their marriage. Amara gave Ejike directions and hung up the phone.

CHAPTER 26

Ejike sped down the highway, constantly glancing at his rearview mirror to make sure he was in the clear. He didn't need any unwanted attention from the police. He was focused on getting to the hospital and being with his wife and son.

He felt a pang of guilt for leaving Amara alone with Obinna in the first place. She had been a real trooper through this all, but to saddle her with the care of Obinna when he went out of town didn't seem fair. Since this ordeal, he looked at her with renewed love and awe. How she was so calm and forgiving was beyond him. Truth be told, if the case was reversed, he wouldn't have an ounce of the grace and class Amara had demonstrated.

God please, let it not be bad. I can't lose another child. I should have handled my business, I know... I know. Please, just cover Obi with Your stripes.

Ejike parked his car and ran across the hospital parking lot. The nurse at the reception desk pointed him to where Nnamdi and Amara sat waiting. They hadn't seen him coming, so he was able to observe Amara. Her arms were folded across her chest. She shook her head from side to side. His heart constricted as he forced his mind to focus on the taking control of the situation and taking the burden off of her.

"Amara..." he called softly.

She stood and walked into his outstretched arms. Her tears quickly soaked through his shirt. After a couple of moments, she freed herself from his embrace. There were no words spoken. He got the feeling that Obinna's illness had opened up a Pandora's Box of emotions within her.

"Thanks for being here for her," Ejike said to Nnamdi, who had come to stand by them.

"No *wahala*. I have to get back to my office, but a doctor will be out to talk to you shortly." The men shook hands, and Nnamdi left.

"Have you heard from Chinelo?" Ejike ushered Amara to the chairs in the corner of the waiting room.

"Yes, I was finally able to get her. She had just landed, so is on her way," Amara said.

"Baby, I'm so sorry—"

"This is not the time or the place. Let's just concentrate on Obinna. The doctor should be out shortly."

Just as she said, a few minutes later, a doctor and a nurse came out to speak with them. Obinna had been given some pain medication to ease his discomfort. They had done some tests and his hemoglobin levels were dangerously low. They needed the permission of a parent to transfuse him.

"Okay, where do I need to sign?" Ejike asked.

"The nurse will show you the way." The doctor said to Ejike. Then he paused and turned to Amara. "Ma'am, you can come with me. He's asking for his mother."

The doctor started to walk away, but Amara's feet remained planted. Ejike saw the anguish on her face. He placed his hand on the small of her back to nudge her forward. Amara remained frozen.

"Where is my son?"

All three of them turned around to see Chinelo. She was panting like she had been running for miles. "Where is Obinna?"

"Are you his mother?" The doctor asked Chinelo.

"Yes…"

"Then follow me."

Chinelo followed without a backward glance.

Amara plopped down on the chair and put her face in her hands. Ejike ached at her pain, torn between either going to sign for the transfusion or comforting his wife. He chose the latter.

He looked up to the waiting nurse. "His mother can give permission for the transfusion. I'll be there shortly.

He pulled Amara into his arms.

CHINELO KNEW WHAT TO EXPECT, but actually seeing it did something to her heart every time. Just like many times before, Obinna had a clip on his finger to monitor his oxygen and heart rate, an oxygen mask, and an IV for hydration and the transfusion. He hadn't had an episode in almost two months. Chinelo was aware that his symptoms could kick in at any time, but she had been following the doctor's orders about his diet and hydration.

"Doctor, how is he?"

"Don't be alarmed. He's resting comfortably now and the blood we'll give him will make him feel a lot better." The doctor walked over to adjust something at the head of the bed.

"How serious is it this time? Did anything in particular trigger it?"

What did Amara do to my son?

"Every episode is different as you must be aware." He paused. "It was a good thing the woman he came with brought him here just in time."

For the next ten minutes, the doctor explained to Chinelo what she had heard so many times before.

He picked up Obinna's chart. "Ma'am, his hematologist was at a conference out of town, but we were able to speak to her." He checked off something on the paper and paused. "She told us you were considering a bone marrow transplant. It'll be in your best interest to make a decision fast. It has some risks, but it's your sure fire bet of relieving him of all this trouble." He placed the clipboard back and walked out of the room.

Chinelo walked over to Obinna. He looked so peaceful. She caressed his cheek with the back of her hand. Tears that had stung the back of her eyes since she got here couldn't be held any longer. She drew the empty chair in the room closer to his bed. She must be the most terrible mother that ever lived. She came to America to get help for her son, but had failed him miserably. Instead of focusing on him, she was busy chasing after a dream that could never be.

She looked up to the ceiling and contemplated talking to Jesus. She dilly-dallied for a moment, and then decided she had nothing to lose at this point.

Jesus, I know I have no right to even call Your name. I've been so terrible that You probably don't want to have anything to do with me...I get it. But please, get Obinna out of this. I have no bargaining chips except to say that I promise to be the best mother there is to him from now on. Even if I abandoned him, which I really didn't mean to—I was just tired and stressed out—You can't abandon him. I get it now. I get it. Seeing him like this has knocked my priorities in the right place. Please soften Ejike and Amara's hearts so he'll agree to be tested.

AMARA LIFTED her eyes to see Chinelo seated in the corner of the waiting room. Her hands were clasped as if in prayer while she rocked back and forth. She had come out of Obinna's room sober, a shadow of herself. At first, Amara didn't want to go in to see him. Not because she didn't care. But because she didn't think she could deal with seeing the boy that she'd had so much fun with days before lie there almost lifeless.

With Ejike by her side, Amara went in to see Obinna. Tears streamed from her eyes when she saw him lying in the bed looking so small and sick. How could she be so selfish? Chinelo had told her about the bone marrow transplant, but she couldn't get over her hurt to give Ejike permission to go ahead and get tested. She would never have refused, but still, she knew her husband needed to actually hear her consent. With so much going on, they had never revisited the issue. She would never forgive herself if something happened to Obinna. He was innocent in all this.

Amara looked over at Ejike. He had been silent for most of the time, but Amara saw his face laced with pain and shame. She wanted to comfort him, but held back. Her emotions were all messed up. She didn't know how she felt towards him. Anger. Sympathy. Hurt. All she knew was that a boy she cared about deeply was in danger and something needed to be done.

"Get tested today," Amara whispered.

Ejike looked at her stunned. "Say that again?"

"I said get tested today. To see if you can be a donor for him." Amara caressed Obinna's face, but didn't look up at Ejike.

"Baby, thank you."

"Don't thank me. I'm not doing this for you or Chinelo. You two brought a boy into my life and have made me care about him. I'm not going to lose him over you guys' foolishness. Get tested today."

Ejike simply nodded.

Several beats of silence passed between them. Amara then stretched out her hands toward Ejike. He placed his hands in hers and they prayed over Obinna.

Obinna stayed in the hospital two more days. When he was ready to be discharged, Chinelo, Amara, and Ejike were all there. They listened as the doctor on call gave them instruction on his care for the next several days. Amara was excited to be taking Obinna home with her. She had cooked his favorite dish and eagerly anticipated the smile on his face when he tasted it.

The hematologist's office had called earlier. The results for the test to see whether Ejike was a match for a bone marrow transplant were in from the lab and she wanted to discuss them. Ejike and Chinelo were headed there as fast as possible to see if they could go ahead with the procedure.

EJIKE GLANCED down at his watch. They had been waiting on the doctor for close to thirty minutes. The last two days had been pure hell. He'd had to deal with his emotions and Amara's. They had barely spoken to each other. Not out of malice, but for lack of appropriate words. Their minds were focused on Obinna. To see the love she had for his son, in spite of the circumstances, put Ejike to shame.

He looked over at Chinelo. Her eyes were closed. In the days since this event, she was a totally different person from the woman he had known all these years. Something seemed to have died in her when she saw Obinna that first day in the hospital. When Amara told Chinelo about her decision for the test, Chinelo's gratitude was expressed through tears. Amara, however, was not moved and she gave Chinelo the same response she gave him. She was doing this for Obinna.

A few moments later, the nurse ushered them into the doctor's office. The look on her face worried Ejike. He had read a lot about bone marrow transplants recently. Even if he wasn't a perfect match, he hoped he would be at least an imperfect match so he could donate.

They exchanged light pleasantries before the doctor pulled out the file. She read it for a few seconds then looked up at them. She took off her glasses and placed them on the table. Ejike's leg began to move up and down unconsciously.

"Ummm... the results came in yesterday..." The doctor began.

She was stalling. Why was she stalling?

Ejike steadied his leg. "Doctor..."

"Does Obinna have any siblings?"

"No," Chinelo said.

"Hmm...okay." The doctor paused. "You were not a match for him, Mr. Dike."

Chinelo let out a heavy sigh and began to sob.

Ejike scooted further toward the desk. "Not even an imperfect match?"

"I'm sorry. No, you weren't." She paused again.

Ejike had the feeling that there was something she wasn't saying. The silence in the room was thick.

"There is something else I have to tell you. According to the results of the test, you are *not* his father."

"Run that by me again," Ejike asked in a raised voice.

The doctor kept quiet and gave him a sympathetic look.

Trembling, Ejike fought against the urge to cry as he thought of Obinna. The boy looked so much like him. How could he not be his son? Ejike's eyes darted to Chinelo. She had stopped crying and was looking at the doctor with her mouth open. Anger welled up inside him as he remembered the baby Amara had lost. Chinelo had cost him so much.

"Chinelo, who is Obinna's real father?"

Fresh tears welled up in Chinelo's eyes. She shook her head. "I don't know."

"That's not going to cut it," he snapped. "I need answers and I need them *now!*"

CHAPTER 27

The doctor must have seen the rage in his eyes because she excused herself and left them alone in the room.

"Talk. Now," Ejike thundered.

"I don't understand it," Chinelo said.

"What don't you understand? The doctor just explained it. A DNA test was done as part of the evaluation and I'm not Obi's father. Should I speak Igbo for you?" Ejike began to pace the small office.

Chinelo shook her head in disbelief. "I'm telling you, Ejike. This has to be a mistake."

"So, you now know better than modern science? You came here with your *wahala* and Obinna is not even mine." Ejike's mind went into overdrive.

He exhaled heavily. "Chinelo, Obinna is not mine, but he looks a lot like me. So that leaves Udo. I knew you guys were close, but did you sleep with him at any time during that window?"

Ejike's cousin, Udo, had always been a charmer and Ejike knew he and Chinelo were friends, but she had Afam. How could she be intimate with all of them in a matter of days?

Chinelo contemplated for a minute. Then she laced her fingers and put her hands on her head. Ejike recognized her surrender. That was all the confirmation he needed.

An hour had passed since the doctor had dealt him that devastating blow. She had come back into the office and given them additional options. They could place Obinna on the registry or have other members of the family tested. By the time Ejike dropped Chinelo off at Gozie's house, he had no more fight left. His rage had subsided and turned into a sense of loss and pain. Chinelo was going to ask Gozie whether he would agree for himself and his eighteen year-old son to be tested.

Ejike pulled his car into the parking space in front of his house. His intention on leaving Gozie's was to drive to Nnamdi's and lament. However, on the way he made a detour to the church. He needed to seek the face of God. He was the only One who could help him sort out this mess. He had prayed and asked for forgiveness all these years for what he had done to Amara, but still, that wasn't enough. He had paid in the end, in a terrible way, too. He not only lost his unborn child they had prayed for, but he nearly lost his home. And it was all for naught.

If God knew that Obinna wasn't his, why did He even let this happen? Why did this disruption have to take place? Why did he have to fall in love with the boy, only to now have him taken away? These were questions that Ejike needed answers to. After an hour of silent prayer in the sanctuary, he picked up one of the Bibles from the pew. Ejike flipped it open, and prayed that the Holy Spirit would speak to him. Tell him how to deal with this from here.

His hands stopped turning the pages at 1 Corinthians 10:3. He read the verse in silence at first, then aloud. *No temptation has overtaken you but such as is common to man; and God is faithful, who will not allow you to be tempted beyond what you are able, but with the temptation will provide the way of escape also, that you may be able to endure it.*

He recited the verse a few more times and a sense of peace

came upon him. Not only had God allowed him to endure, but He kept his marriage intact in the process. At the end of the day, he and Amara had grown and rekindled their love for Christ and each other. The only loser here was Chinelo. He felt sad for her. One thing Ejike knew for sure was that he wanted Obinna to remain in his life. They still shared the same blood. Now all he had to do was convince Amara.

EJIKE WALKED into his home at 6:30 pm. The house was quiet. Amara and Obinna were probably upstairs. He called out Amara's name, but was met with silence. Ejike quietly made his way up the stairs trying not to make noise. He opened the door of his bedroom and his heart welled up at the sight he saw. Amara and Obinna were cuddled on the bed sleeping. Their breathing was inaudible and only visible through the rise and fall of their chests. The door squeaked when he tried to close it, causing them to shift, but they kept sleeping.

His phone buzzed, so he quickly exited the room. He released his phone from the clip on his belt. It was a text from Chinelo. She wanted to know whether they could keep Obinna overnight. She wanted to talk to Gozie alone. Ejike responded with a simple yes. He didn't trust himself to say much more, especially without talking to Amara first.

Ejike went to the kitchen. He hadn't eaten since breakfast. He closed the fridge, turned around, and saw Amara behind him.

He put the plate of leftover Jollof rice in the microwave and set the timer. "I'm sorry. I didn't mean to wake you."

"No worries. I felt really tired for some reason, so Obi and I decided to nap a little. When did you get back?" Amara kissed her husband lightly on the lips.

"Just now." The timer went off and Ejike carried his plate to the dinette while Amara filled a glass with water and brought it to him. She pulled up a chair and sat down next to him.

Ejike blessed his food and began to eat. He watched as Amara studied him closely.

"Soooooo, how did it go?" Amara finally asked.

Ejike set his spoon down and drank some water. "Baby, I have something to tell you."

"What is it? The look on your face is scaring me." Her brows were furrowed.

"Well, remember the sample they took from me was to be used for—"

"Ejike, stop it. Get to the point!" she said.

"I was not a match for Obinna." He paused to let that sink him before he dropped the other bombshell. He could see the disappointment written all over her face. "Apart from that, Obinna is not my son." The words got caught in his throat and were uncomfortable coming out. But it didn't feel half as uncomfortable as Amara looked.

"You say what!!" She stood, hands on her hips. She held on to her stomach. Something about her stance didn't seem right to him. His suspicions were confirmed when she said, "I think I'm going to be sick."

Amara ran to the bathroom. Ejike stood up and followed her. By the time he got there, she was bent over the commode where she emptied the contents of her stomach.

"Are you okay?" Ejike asked.

Amara remained silent. She stood, flushed, and turned to the sink to rinse her mouth.

Ejike's heart ached that he had caused her so much grief. She leaned against the door and folded her arms across her body. In a voice that was barely audible, she said, "Start talking."

～

AMARA PLOPPED down on the chair. With her head in her hands, she could hear Ejike talking, but the words didn't register. Her heartbeat quickened as a tear rolled down her cheek. A million thoughts ran through her mind. She sat in silence. All this pain was for naught? Her loss was just a casualty in Chinelo's sick game. How could she sleep with three men in the same time frame? Udo? Her mind never would have gone there.

"Amara, I'm so, so sorry for the pain you've had to go through and the loss of our baby."

Amara turned away from Ejike. She didn't want to remember. The betrayal cut deep. As much as she wanted to remain angry, she knew it would just hurt the more. In the last few weeks, she had done a lot to try to accept the situation. In Jesus, she had found the strength and grace to deal with it. Besides, thinking about it would pull her far back to that place of anger.

"What will happen to Obinna now?" Amara asked.

"Chinelo will ask Gozie to be tested."

She felt Ejike hands on her knees and he stooped down in front of her. "God has been faithful to us. He helped us to weather this storm. I don't know how you did it, but you forgave me. Please find it in your heart to forgive your cousin, too."

The words that he spoke sunk in. "Forgive her?" Amara asked. "Are you kidding me?"

"Babe, I'm the one who you should be mad at. I betrayed our commitment. I'm the one that owed you allegiance. If Chinelo got in the middle of it, it's because I let her. I made a bad choice. But the issue here is that an innocent child has been dragged into this."

"What are you getting at?" Amara looked at him with confusion in her eyes.

"Obinna may not be mine, but he is blood. I want him to remain in our lives." Ejike studied her.

Amara knew that he was waiting for a reaction, but right now she was numb. One thing was certain, the love she had for Obinna had crept up on her while she wasn't looking. Part of her wanted to breathe a sigh of relief that he wasn't Ejike's. Their lives would go back to normal. As she thought it, she knew that things could never be as they were. Despite that fact that Obinna wasn't his, Ejike had experienced what it was like to father a child. Her relief was mixed with despair at what this meant for them.

"Ejike, I've accepted Obi as your son. So accepting him as Udo's son is not a problem. My problem is I have suffered so much. I lost my baby for nothing. Obi is not even yours."

God surely knew that this was too much to bear. After all, she was human and not a saint. Her anger rose in that instant. She needed time to think.

"Ejike, I can't process what you're asking me. I just can't." She stood, went upstairs to their bedroom, and closed the door.

Amara pulled back the covers and got into the queen-sized bed in the guest room. She lay there motionless while her tears flowed freely. *I was doing good, Lord. I had started to forgive. I had tried to push through the pain. But this isn't fair. I lost my child because of the shock of finding out Ejike had a child...but he really didn't? How am I supposed to let go of this? Or forgive Chinelo for not getting her facts straight. Or Ejike for even giving her this opportunity at all. For years, I begged You to allow me to conceive, then I do and You allow this to happen. Again for nothing??*

She rubbed her stomach and sobbed. A sense of calm washed over her as she remembered what her mother always told her after dealing with scorn from her father's younger wife. She'd say, "I will hold on to my God, for in my weakness, enduring insults and trials, He remains perfect and His grace is sufficient enough for me." It was her mother's version of 2 Corinthians 12, verses 9 and 10 where Paul was willing to suffer for the sake of Christ.

Suddenly, Amara realized that what she was going through didn't hold a candle to what her mother went through. She sat up. She wasn't making excuses for Ejike, and they would need counseling, but she loved her husband and she knew he loved her. She wasn't willing to let her marriage fall apart. Amara knew him standing up to his mother in her favor was no easy feat. Now it was her turn to stand with him in his pain. She might never be able to give him a child. Obinna was as good as he was going to get. Unless they agreed on adoption.

She started for the door. As she turned the handle, she came face to face with Ejike. He studied her, his apprehension visible. She gave him a faint smile. The next thing she knew, she was being wrapped in the safety of his arms.

CHAPTER 28

With the dawning of a new day, Amara was now certain that she had lost her mind. She tried to remember what she must have been on when she agreed with Ejike that Chinelo should come to their house so they could all talk.

Some time during the night, Chinelo had sent a text saying Gozie had agreed that he and his oldest son would get tested. That made them both happy. They had spent the better part of the night talking about their proposal to Chinelo and how it would all work out. They wanted Chinelo to let Obinna stay with them during the summer. They also decided that at this point there would be no need to confuse the boy with any specifics about his paternity. Telling him that Afam was his stepdad and Ejike was his real father, and now having to tell him about Udo would be too much for a five year-old boy to comprehend.

Amara tore a paper towel off the roll and dried her hands. It was a mid-August and hot, but she had a taste for some goat meat pepper soup. Her stomach still felt funny. Might have been something she ate.

She placed pieces of white boiled yam into a bowl and covered them with her soup. Moving to the living room, she propped her feet up and turned on the television. She flipped through the channels, and finally landed on her favorite, The Food Network. She smiled when she saw the Neely's. She loved all the cooking shows, but really loved to see a black couple cooking and having fun with it.

Amara was awakened by keys turning in the lock. She glanced at the clock that hung on the wall. She couldn't believe she had slept for an hour. The door opened and Obinna came rushing in.

"Is mommy here yet?" Obinna asked, running to Amara.

"No, she isn't. Soon. Did you have fun?"

"Yes." Obinna spent the next few minutes telling her about his escapades with daddy and Uncle Nnamdi at Home Depot and the toy store.

"Hey, you," Ejike said, flipping through the mail. His eyes saw her almost empty bowl and his expression changed. The yam was gone but there a couple pieces of goat meat left.

Ejike popped a piece of meat in his mouth. "You waited for me to leave before you prepared this delicacy?"

She smiled. "Are you hungry? Didn't you stop to eat something?"

Ejike ignored her and walked to the kitchen.

She laughed out loud. "Leave my kitchen alone, oh. Lunch will be ready when you get back down."

LUNCH WAS DONE and the kitchen was tidied up by the time the knock they expected came. It took little or no effort for Obinna to fall asleep for a nap. Timely too, since that would give them the much needed privacy to talk.

Ejike squeezed her hand for a quick second and proceeded down the hallway to the door. Moments later Amara heard voices in a low whisper. Her heart beat against her chest a little faster.

This is my house. She should be the one scared.

However, Amara knew that she wasn't scared of Chinelo, but the possibility of how this conversation could go down if Chinelo decided to be aggressive. Amara had prayed for Holy Spirit to be present in her speech and countenance. It was only by the way she acted that Chinelo would hopefully get to see Christ.

As they approached, Amara recited Mathew 5:16, *In the same way, let your light shine before others, that they may see your good deeds and glorify your Father in heaven.* She had recited that verse so many times in the last thirteen hours, it was ridiculous.

Chinelo and Ejike entered the room. Amara stayed seated. Her eyes studied Chinelo. She seemed to have aged or maybe it was her conscience eating at her. Amara quickly felt the Holy Spirit convict her.

"Amara, *kedu?* How are you?" Chinelo sat on the chair opposite Amara.

"I'm good. Where is brother Gozie? I thought he was coming with you."

"He dropped me off. He had some business to handle. He'll be back a little later." Chinelo looked around the house, probably looking for Obinna.

"Obi's sleeping upstairs. He had a real busy morning,'" Amara said.

"Oh, okay," Chinelo said.

Her answer was followed by an awkward silence. Ejike took the seat by Amara. Amara remembered when laughter and gist passing back and forth between them was their normal. Right now, that seemed like so many moons ago. The atmosphere felt thick and foggy, as they all sat there in silence.

Then Chinelo spoke. "I didn't think. Not for one moment did I entertain the thought that Udo could be Obinna's dad. I mean it was just one night." Tears rolled down Chinelo's face.

"Tears? You can't be serious. You can't use those tears to get out of this one," Ejike said. "Wasn't it just one night with me? How did you conclude he was mine?"

"I guess somewhere deep down, I wanted him to be yours. It was my last chance of getting your attention."

"Why?" Amara and Ejike asked in unison.

"At what cost?" Ejike asked.

Amara remained silent, waiting for answers. None were forthcoming. She turned to Ejike. Her blood began to rise again. As much as she tried to do the Christian thing, listening to them talk about their one night stand wasn't really her thing.

There was an awkward silence before Chinelo continued. "I'm sorry. I don't what I can do to show that I'm sorry."

Amara met Ejike's stare. She nodded her head slightly, authorizing him to go ahead.

"There is one thing," Ejike said.

"What?" Chinelo looked up. Her eyes darted from Amara to Ejike. "*O gini?*"

"Since Udo and his parents died in the same plane crash, I'm the only family Obinna has on his father's side." He paused and squeezed Amara's hand, then continued. "We would like to remain in touch with him. Not just through phone calls, but we'd want him to come and spend summers here with us."

"You and Amara want Obinna to come here during the summer?" Chinelo asked, clearly puzzled at the gesture.

"Yes." Ejike confirmed.

"Why?" Chinelo's raised eyebrows told Amara that she still wasn't convinced there wasn't a catch.

"I just told you. We're his only family on his dad's side and we have grown to love him."

Amara could feel Chinelo's stare penetrate her skin. This wasn't easy for her, but the fact was, she did love Obinna and her husband needed this. Especially since she couldn't give him a son of his own. Ejike turned and looked at her. It dawned on her that they were waiting for her to say something.

"Yes, we would like him to spend the summers with us," Amara confirmed.

"What kind of people are you?"

"Meaning?" Ejike asked.

"I mean, I come here with a totally different motive that nearly destroyed you. And you virtually turn the other cheek. Being in the hospital with Obi at the worst he's ever been has taught me that life is fickle. I want to know about Jesus, but there's no way I can do what both of you are doing. There's absolutely no way." Chinelo shook her head.

This was a chance Amara had been waiting for. Despite everything, she knew she must be about her Father's business. Amara spoke to Ejike, prompted by the Holy Spirit, "Honey, can you go and check on Obinna? I want to speak to Chinelo alone."

Ejike's expression asked her why. She rubbed the back of this hand, reassuring him that it was okay. Ejike stood and headed cautiously toward the stairs. She gave him a reassuring smile and stood to sit closer to Chinelo.

"Chi," Amara said, calling her by her nickname to ease the tension between them.

Chinelo stared at her in silence.

"When all this went down, I was hurt and angry and questioned God. Why should something like this happen to me? I go to church, I pray, I pay my tithes and offering. Surely I deserved to be blessed with my heart's desires - a child being at the top of that list. But instead of giving me one, He gives my husband one through my own cousin." Amara paused in time to see Chinelo flinch.

Amara continued, "I thought everything was by my power and might, but if it hadn't been for His sustaining grace, I couldn't have survived the pain. His grace sought me out, and kept me secure when I felt like I was all alone. It sanctified me in a way that I was able to open my heart to try and work things out. I thought my life was over. But then I saw how blessed I was. Not many Nigerian men would give up a son to keep a barren wife. That is the favor of God. Not many can boast of the kind of man I have.

So I got to thinking, that grace and love that is given to me so freely, I should be able to give an ounce of it to someone else..."

"Me? I don't deserve anything good from you. If I were you, I would have kicked my behind a long time ago."

"You see it that way because as humans, the love we extend to one another is conditional. But God's love isn't."

"Amara, I'm so sorry about everything, but are you sure you're okay with Obinna coming here?"

"Yes. I love Obinna and I'll do anything for my husband and this is what he wants. Besides having Obinna around is a plus. He's a delightful young man."

"So wipe the slate clean just like that? I find it difficult coming to terms with this your kindness," Chinelo said.

Amara smiled. "My forgiveness isn't about you. It's about me and following the commandments of God."

"And you have peace?" Chinelo asked, tears in her eyes.

"Why are you crying?"

"Because I'm tired of chasing happiness around and nothing coming of it."

"You don't need to chase happiness. You need joy and only Christ can give that to you," Amara said with a smile.

They heard running and looked up to see Ejike and Obinna coming down the stairs. Obinna ran to his mother. Amara suspected that this was the longest they had stayed away from each other. While mother and son got reacquainted, Amara motioned Ejike to follow her to the kitchen.

In the kitchen, Amara filled Ejike in on her talk with Chinelo. The expression on his face softened. He cupped her face in his hands, looked deeply into her eyes, and said, "I love and adore you, Amara. For years, I was afraid that once you knew about that night, I would have to know what it's like to live without you. Not only do I not have to go through that horrible experience, you have set aside your pain to make me happy. I don't know what I did to deserve you, but I'll spend the rest of my days making it up to you."

Amara stood on her toes to plant a kiss on his lips. He wrapped his arms around her, and pulled her close.

"I love you, too, and I'm not some kind of superhero. It is by His grace that I am what I am."

Ejike looked down at her. With one arm still wrapped around her, he lifted her head with his index finger. "Apart from my salvation, God must love me extra by giving me you."

Ejike's lips connected with hers.

EPILOGUE

It was a sunny and bright Sunday morning. Through the stained glass, Amara could see the trees moving from side to side under the effect of the blustering winds. Amara adjusted her gold *gele*. She was going to opt for an English attire, but it was a special day—the day that the Lord had made—so she decided to go all out. Her single-arm, gold blouse matched the purple and gold velveteen wrapper that was made for her straight from Nigeria. Not that there weren't fantastic tailors in Dallas, but her mother wanted to oversee this outfit herself. This was a special event.

She glanced to her side. Ejike held Chima on his lap and Obinna was on his other side. Chinelo sat on the other end of the pew, in between her brother and a gentleman she called, "a friend."

Amara felt Ejike's eyes on her. She met his stare. He smiled. She did the same. They had been through a lot in the past fifteen months, but had weathered the storm. Through prayer and counseling, they held on the best they knew how and worked hard to regain some normalcy in their marriage.

Gozie didn't turn out to be a match for Obinna, but his oldest son did—although, it took some convincing for him to agree to do the bone marrow transplant.

One night, right before Obinna was to undergo the procedure, Ejike announced that if Amara was willing to try adoption, so was he. Amara went through a range of emotions. Joy. Fear. Relief. But she didn't want to commit to anything 'til Obinna was in the clear. The procedure was a resounding success and Obinna's health had markedly improved.

A month into the adoption process, Amara went to see the doctor for flu related symptoms. It was during that visit that she got the best news of her life—she was pregnant. Amara and Ejike had been so busy with the adoption and taking turns sleeping at the hospital with Obinna that she had neglected to see all the signs. It also didn't help that they had given up any hope of becoming parents naturally. They decided to proceed with the adoption of the then six month-old baby boy—Chima James Dike. They decided to name him Chima meaning, "God knows," because He alone knew why she and Ejike had to go through what they did.

After months of recuperation and follow-up doctor visits, Chinelo and Obinna left for Nigeria. Chinelo decided not to let Obinna return for the following summer to give Amara and Ejike some time to repair their marriage—alone. Amara appreciated her gesture of atonement and was overjoyed when Chinelo told her she had committed her life to Jesus. They did, however, stay in touch with Obinna via Skype and phone calls. It was overwhelming seeing the almost seven year-old boy again. He had grown so much and the resemblance to Udo was uncanny.

Pastor Harris' voice interrupted her thoughts.

"Now it's the part of the service we've been waiting for. The Dikes are no strangers to this church. They have been faithful servants of God and He has decided to bless them with a precious gift."

The applause was loud and went on for at least two minutes.

Then the pastor continued, "Family, this goes to show you that we have a promise-keeping God. He may not be on your time schedule, but He is on the perfect time schedule…His. Please stand on your feet while I ask the Dike's to bring forward their bundle of joy, so we can pray over them."

Amara stood up and secured her wrapper, then reached over to her nanny who handed over her five month-old baby. The infant's big, brown eyes were a replica of her father's. Amara mouthed a "thank you" to the heavens.

Amara waited while Ejike properly balanced Chima with one arm and held Obinna's hand with the other. Chinelo, her friend, Eric, and her brother Gozie, stood all around them.

"Where are her godparents?" Pastor Harris asked.

"We're here," Tonye and David said in unison, moving to the front.

The pastor raised his hands. "Father in heaven, as You have given her to us, we dedicate her back to You. Give her parents and godparents the ability to raise her and her brother in the way that is pleasing to You. May they be proper custodians of the gifts You have given them in Jesus' name. Amen." There was applause.

"Church, I present to you Ogechi Victoria Dike," Pastor Harris said.

Ogechi: God's time. Despite the hurt and pain, amazing things happened when Amara leaned on the grace of God for the ability to let go.

Yes, God's time was the best and Amara was grateful for the grace to wait on it.

THE END

DISCUSSION QUESTIONS

1. Chinelo thought that Obinna's illness was punishment for her wayward ways. Do you ever think illness is a punishment for anything when the blood of Jesus has paid the price?

2. Amara sought medical help for her infertility. Does that make her faithless in God's ability to change her situation around?

3. Ejike's betrayal took place during his break from Amara. Does that make him any less guilty of infidelity?

4. Ejike thought Amara was too naïve. Remember the verse "Be wise as serpents but as gentle as doves"? What is your interpretation of that verse? Do you agree with Ejike or was he just trying to justify his deeds?

5. Was Chinelo right to keep Obinna a secret? Did she use him as a pawn in her quest to hang onto the past?

6. At first Amara didn't kick Ejike out until she talked to Chinelo and found out there was more? How much is too much when it comes to betrayal?

7. Amara was of the opinion that paying her tithes and offerings, going to church and being faithful was her "sacrifice" for her "reward" which was a good man—Ejike. Do we sometimes believe that the favor and grace of God is given as a result of something we have done?

8. Did you support the Dike's decision in regards to Obinna after the paternity test results were reveled? Why or why not?

Millions of people are in need of a bone marrow transplant either for themselves or a loved one. Consider joining the registry or spreading the word. It could save a life. As always consult your doctor before making any medical decisions.

www.bethematch.org

Thank you for reading.

Final Note

Thank you for reading Amara & Ejike's story. Please consider leaving a review on the platform you purchased the book. I greatly appreciate honest feedback.

If you liked this story, I trust you might like some of my other titles. But before we get to those, never miss a sale, new release announcements, or freebies. You can ensure that by joining my mailing list. I'd love to stay connected.

Pretend Bae

Away To Africa

New Year's Kiss (Prequel)

Rent-A-Bae